Tamanna
A True Story of Forbidden Love

TEJESHWAR SINGH

FiNGERPRINT!

Published by

FiNGERPRINT!

An imprint of Prakash Books India Pvt. Ltd.

113/A, Darya Ganj, New Delhi-110 002,
Tel: (011) 2324 7062 – 65, Fax: (011) 2324 6975
Email: info@prakashbooks.com/sales@prakashbooks.com

facebook www.facebook.com/fingerprintpublishing
twitter www.twitter.com/FingerprintP, www.fingerprintpublishing.com
For manuscript submissions, e-mail: fingerprintsubmissions@gmail.com

ISBN: 978 81 7234 529 7

Processed & printed in India by HT Media Ltd., Noida

To you, dear Tamanna. The debt of gratitude
still remains on me.

ACKNOWLEDGEMENTS

I would like to thank:

Dr. Daisaku Ikeda, my mentor, my guide. You resurrected my life from the ashes in 2007. I owe it to you, Sensei.

My two moms, Sarla and Sarla, because of whom I could live day to day, maintain my dignity, and remain alive.

My Seraph, my heart, my wife, Heena, who has crossed all boundaries to sustain me.

To my Angel, my heart, my daughter, Sakhi, whose innocent prayers are with me forever.

Will I ever be able to pay back my debt of gratitude to you all?

This book is the journey of my emotions and everything that I felt for love—every feeling that I experienced right from the day I met her to the day I saw her last.

It is an attempt by me to accept the truth of the mysterious workings of the human heart.

AUTHOR SPEAKS

Love is always pure and sacred. It is an evolution process in itself. It can unravel all the mysteries of the universe. True happiness in love has no parallel. It is a state that can never be fully explained. It can only be experienced, and is divine.

Fall in love and you will find out the Truth.

Every fiction is a reality that must have happened somewhere at some point of time. After all, reality and fiction are two sides of the same coin: each reality is a story, and each story a reality.

This work of fiction is no different: it is my story, my reality. The characters of this book—Arjun, Sangini, and Tamanna—exist in this very universe. The content inside this book happened to me. The events in this story took place in my life, majorly between the years 2007 and 2009.

So why have I written it as a work of fiction, you ask? Because, this book is not hundred percent true. I had to add some fiction to my story to meet the demands of publishing and editing. While at some places I condensed a lengthy conversation to a few lines, at others I skipped some events that did not add much value to the text. But I took care to not make any significant changes to the reality. The building remains the same. I just removed some extra bricks from it.

I wrote this book in a fragile and mysterious condition, one that I feel is beyond the limited understanding of the human mind. I, myself, could not comprehend it. Once I started writing, I couldn't stop. A maddening urge pushed me forward, word by word, line after line. I did not need to think; my feelings guided my pen as and when I sat down to write.

The only thing I knew was that something extraordinary was happening to me. It made me realise that human life is a great work of fiction, unpredictable and undoubtedly designed by a higher power, a power that manifests itself in the mysteries of love and desire.

EDITOR SPEAKS

Edit a great love story, a pure love story, and you will marvel at the mysteries of human emotions and behaviour. A lot has been said and written about love, but even then, a lot remains unsaid and unwritten ...

One day, I got a phone call from Usha Sood, a family friend. She is the principal of a reputable Delhi school. I was busy, but I couldn't avoid the call. Usha is a dear friend, and I respect her a lot. I asked about her health and then enquired about the purpose of her call. She told me she had been approached by a young woman in her office some days back with an unpublished manuscript.

"I have never heard that kind of a confident voice before," she said. "I have never seen that kind of courage before. I am not easily impressed, but there was something about her aura that invoked immense respect. She had a tall frame of about 5'8", a shining, fair complexion, and a beautifully crafted face. She wore a white suit and sported a big red bindi on her forehead. Smiling sadly, she came to me with a bunch of papers. She said she wanted to get that story published. It was written by her husband."

"Written by her husband? Was he with her?" I asked. Even though I was busy, I was slightly intrigued.

"No, he was not," Usha replied. "When I asked her about him, she smiled. Her eyes shone brilliantly. Her spotless face didn't betray it, but even then I could vaguely feel that she was engulfed in remorse. 'My husband is the most wonderful person I have ever known in my life. And I must help him now,' she said. 'He has seen enough in life and has fought valiantly. Now it is my time to fight for him. This is the biggest test of my life, a new aspect of human life that destiny wants me to understand. It is not easy for me. But still, I would never allow him to live in guilt. He must never suffer out of shame. I want the world to know the complete truth.' She sighed deeply, fighting back tears. Before I could reply, she got up and walked out of the office, leaving behind the manuscript on my table."

"That is weird. Did you read the book?" I asked.

"Wait, there's more. After she left, I called my friend through whom this woman had come. I narrated the whole incident to her. She gave me a straightforward answer. 'Usha, I have great respect for her. She is trustworthy and categorically asked me to help without asking any questions. And I respect her request. I can vouch for her anytime. Please help her.'

"I disconnected the phone and looked at the bundle of pages on my table. They seemed to be calling out to me. Curious, I picked them up and started reading the book . . . and I couldn't stop. By the end, I had tears in my eyes. It's a beautiful tale of love . . . you must publish this book. This story must be told to the world."

It seemed like I finally had a great love story to edit . . .

ARJUN SPEAKS

I love you, Sangini.

Ohhh, for you my soul always sings songs. You are in every ounce of my being. I love you, I always have, and I will continue to love you till my last breath. You are my love, my very reason of existence, and my desire to live. So much I love you that I never want to depart alone from this world, leaving you behind. You are the treasure of my life.

But still, I had to do what I had to do, for a selfish motive—to remain healthy and alive. The pages of this book are my priest, to whom I am confessing all my sins and secrets. What a strange situation destiny has landed me into.

Some questions have haunted me these past years. Am I a faithful man? Have I led a regret-free life? Have I loved somebody absolutely truthfully? Even today I don't know the answers. All I know is that I have always walked on the path of humanism.

We all stand naked in front of our inner conscience. We can't fool ourselves. I, too, know about my truth. Love offered me a great chance to experience a much deeper insight into the mysteries of my heart, which houses a loving husband, a caring father, a dutiful son, a sincere friend . . . and a confused lover of Tamanna.

Tamanna . . . It was not an ordinary attraction. Initially, I fought against it, but my emotions continued to grow and take phenomenal proportions. When I look back at it now, I realise that it was an extraordinarily mysterious experience. I don't know why it happened or how it happened. But it happened, and that is the undisputable truth.

I could have chosen to behave as if nothing was happening to me and life would have moved on with its usual routine. I could have kept the truth of my love inside my heart forever, but I couldn't.

How could I have ignored my emotions when I was getting up in the middle of the night in a semi-conscious state and typing feverishly on my mobile phone? I would barely remember what I typed during that mystical state the next morning. But it would all become clear when I would open the Notes app on my mobile. I was composing poem after poem for Tamanna. I was typing out my most unedited emotions and feelings for her.

The game of destiny eventually resulted in my getting psychiatric advice to write down everything. Otherwise I might have suffered from some serious neurological disorder.

Don't get me wrong, Sangini. I am no womaniser, my love. My conscience is crystal clear. I never desired Tamanna physically. My love for her was pure and platonic. And it never lessened my love for you.

So why did I never confide in you? Because I was clueless, lost, confused. I didn't want to hurt you. I didn't want all this to happen. But I could not help it either. I am not a coward and you know that. Even today, the only reason why I am pouring my heart out is that I want to stay alive and in senses, for you and our daughter.

You know how they say that real life is extraordinary? I realise its truth today, sitting at my study table, writing these pages, guided by my higher self to document the greatest mystery of my heart. There is a heavy debt on my soul. And by putting the truth of my heart on these pages, I am trying to ease the burden of that debt.

I need my peace. Hence, I must share everything truthfully.

I love you, Sangini.

PROLOGUE

It was 5.30 a.m. I was waiting outside Tamanna's house in a borrowed car. I needed a car with tinted windows to make sure no one saw me.

Inside the car I was trying to smile like her, trying to move my lips like her. This was my way of keeping her with me. On the stereo, a Meera Bai *bhajan* was playing. Meera Bai, the greatest lover of all times. My pen drive was full of her love-soaked *bhajans*. I was looking towards her home, mouthing the lyrics, my eyes famished for a glance of her. I waited.

More than one hour passed. It was now 6.45 a.m. She came out every day at this time, to wait with her son for the school bus. But not today . . .

How could she? She was thousands of miles away.

Yet, I waited.

I was dejected, shattered. With tears in my eyes, I again tried to smile like her and whispered, "I am going to Chandigarh. Will meet you soon. Bye."

I had a business meeting to attend in Chandigarh, and for that I was dressed in a white shirt, black tie, grey jacket, and black jeans. She loved black denims, and it was all I had been wearing for months now. This was another way I was keeping her with me.

It had been three months since I last heard her voice. The longest three months of my life.

Each day, I'd woken up with the hope that she would call up that day and I'd get a chance to apologise, to say how dearly I wanted her to be in my life, to tell her that she was one of the most precious persons in my life.

Ever since she'd left for Finland, my heart had urged me to go around her house. *Maybe she would come out in her balcony and you would get a glimpse of her*, my heart would say to me. I constantly thought of passing through the lane where she lived and being able to touch her car, touch the latch of her front door, things she would have touched every day. At that time, that was the only way I could feel her presence.

Each day for the past three months, I had wanted her a thousand times more than the previous day.

The great hurricane of love makes even the wisest people helpless. When one is in love, one often goes overboard in life. The strong winds of love overpower the mind, so much so that one fails to distinguish between right and wrong. Oh love! Love!

Feelings make us behave most unpredictably. We are left with just one resounding desire in our mind: *I want that person. I want that person in my life.*

The same happened with me. The very mention of her name made my knees go weak. Her thoughts gave me goose bumps. Her voice resounded in my mind all the time.

"Tamanna . . . I-I love you," I murmured.

But she was not there. She was nowhere near me. But despite that I fumbled while saying those three magical words.

This experience was new for me. In a way, I was exploring the vast expanse of my emotional state. It was my newest side, an adventure into the uncharted territories of my mind.

With tears in my eyes, I turned on the ignition and started my journey to Chandigarh. The last time I had made that journey was in Oct 2009, shortly before my last phone call to Tamanna. After that phone call, I suffered a nervous breakdown and was taken to PGIMER Chandigarh by Babbu, my best friend. There I met Dr Harpal Singh, my psychiatrist.

Twelve days ago, on 3rd Jan, 2010, the day Tamanna left for Helsinki, I suffered my last bout of depression. Till that day, I had been praying to God to help me cope with all the confusion and pain of missing Tamanna every single second. Both Sangini and I were ardent followers of Buddhism, and we prayed daily for more peace and wisdom. But that day even my prayers did not work. I broke down while saying them. All that was going on in my overloaded mind was that I may never see Tamanna again.

To my good fortune, Sangini had gone to her mother's place that day. I immediately called up Dr Harpal and shared everything with him. During the last two months, I had spoken to him on a couple of occasions and had developed a friendly rapport with him. We spoke for over an hour, during which he advised me to write down on paper all the unsaid words I had in my heart for Tamanna.

Following his suggestion, I thought of writing a letter to her—a letter that would never reach her. With moist eyes and trembling hands, I started writing.

Dear Tamanna,

How are you?
My apologies, first of all, for writing to you in this manner. I have no choice as all my attempts to talk to you and convey to you what I really feel have failed miserably. I was, and still am, astonished and perturbed as

to how a beautiful relationship became so painful. Well, I guess, it was an exquisite dream that had to end one day.

It was all quite strange. Ever since I met you, I always felt connected to you by some strong and mysterious force. I would try very hard to stay away from you. But each time I would fail pathetically.

I've never had this kind of connection with anyone else before. Even with Sangini, I fell in love gradually. And I love her immensely—I always have. But you came into my life like the first drops of rain on a parched earth.

You always seemed to be my own. I felt a sense of belonging with you. I couldn't define my feelings, it was sheer magnetism. I was drawn very, very strongly to you.

Over the weeks, I realised I loved you. I thought non-stop about you. I tried to push back my emotions, but I could never succeed. We talked to each other, we laughed and had fun over the phone. All this made me very happy. Your conversations were very encouraging. You always appreciated my book and inspired me to write more, as if you wanted nothing but my success and happiness. I was overwhelmed. You too liked talking to me, at least I felt that way. All in all, it was magically intoxicating.

When and how my feelings resulted in a book of verses, I have no clue. I wrote all of them in a condition I still do not understand. It was a most mystical experience.

I respect you for what you are. I hold you in high esteem as you have always been true to your husband. You have always been so dignified.

Then the inevitable happened around three months back. You misunderstood my point of view. I wanted to talk to you one last time and properly explain the truth of my heart. I called you repeatedly, but your attitude was hard-hearted. It seemed like you were accusing and ridiculing me. I felt as if I was some roadside playboy who was chasing you for cheap thrills and you just wanted to get rid of me.

During our last conversation, you repeatedly said, "I don't want to talk about anything. You be in your world and do your duties." Well,

I have been doing exactly that. Just that I really wanted to talk to you and tell you the truth. I was not scared of your reaction. What could you do? Push me away? Slap me? I would have gladly accepted that. Even today, I say, please disrespect me, insult me, hurt me, curse me. After all, I have dared to love a married woman. Please hate me for doing that, torment me, but listen to me first—that was all I ever had in my mind.

When you did not answer my calls, all my realisations, my repentance, all the regard that I had for you, went for a toss. Here I was trying to come to terms with myself and losing you, and there you were completely avoiding me. It hurt terribly to be abandoned in a second by a woman who had showed so much attachment and concern towards me. From a trusted confidante, I suddenly become an untouchable, left to die. I went through the most horrible phase of my life. I became angry. I hated and cursed myself for falling in love with a married woman. Physically, my body suffered for more than a month. I am still trying to regain my health. I will take my time, but I know I will come around. I am determined. I can't afford to lose myself. I have responsibilities towards my wife and my daughter.

Our relationship was beautiful, Tamanna, and I didn't want it to end bitterly. Our time together was my strength. It was love in its purest form. I never ever thought of causing misery to you or your husband. I considered your family mine. I worried for you and your son. And I assure you that because of me you will never have to look down and be embarrassed before your husband. I unintentionally fell in love with you. It just happened! I am sorry.

I am not a home-breaker. I don't keep falling for women. Oh my God. I don't know why it happened with you. I am trying very hard to get you out of my mind, my heart, my soul. I promise to never cross the path you walk on . . .

Be happy. Don't even think about this double-faced man who forgot all his duties and fell in love with you like an adolescent boy. Don't *worry, I have strangulated that boy inside the closed confines of my heart forever.*

Warmth,
Arjun

After the massive outpour, I felt much better. My ever-present headache suddenly disappeared. I felt as If I'd found a way out of my misery. It didn't matter to me even an ounce whether my feelings had any audience or not.

That letter was the beginning of a journey to explore the hidden aspects of my soul, to go deep into the ocean of my life and note down its secret and baffling treasures.

This book is the outcome of that unparalleled, life-changing journey of love.

1

I met Tamanna for the first time in February 2007 at the birthday party of our neighbours' three-year-old daughter. Sangini and I had met the easygoing couple, Vipin and Pinky Makhija, only three months back during one of our daily morning walks in a nearby park. Both husband and wife were friendly and sweet, so despite the fact that I was depressed and was not keen on making new acquaintances, we started exchanging *hellos* and *good mornings* and, over time, began talking casually. Then one morning, they invited us to their daughter's birthday party and insisted that we come. Unwilling to disappoint them, Sangini and I decided to go. It was the first time we were visiting their home.

At the party, after giving the birthday girl our blessings and her birthday gift, Sangini and I walked to one corner of the hall to stand and eat snacks. Sangini began to talk about how beautiful Makhijas' home was. I listened inattentively, nodding and smiling at the right places and noticing other guests. A minute later, my eyes fell upon a young woman who was sitting towards my left. She had seated the little birthday girl on her lap and was showering wishes on her. She seemed extremely sincere, simple, and loving. Even Sangini noticed her and appreciated her demeanour. She wasn't extraordinarily beautiful but she was definitely the most attractive woman I'd ever seen. Something stirred inside me the moment I saw her. Her smile, her eyes, and her entire aura affected me very deeply. I felt a sudden surge of happiness inside me.

I kept stealing glances at her from time to time. She was wearing a well-fitted pair of black jeans and a yellow cotton top that was just about covering her belt. She looked humble and stylish at the same time. Her tall frame was strikingly similar to Sangini's. She was not very fair but had a spotless glowing complexion. Her long hair complimented her full, well-maintained figure, and her big beautiful eyes looked even prettier with her naturally curved eye lashes. A plump, heavy man stood at her side. I heard him asking the hosts about the drinks arrangement. I thought he was kidding; after all it was a party for kids. But apparently he was not joking.

Some minutes later, Vipin and Pinky ushered the woman and this man to our corner. We were introduced to each other. The woman, of course, was Tamanna Sahni, and the man was her husband, Sanjay. I was a little sad to know that the beautiful woman was married and sadder to know that her husband was an impolite, overweight man.

Tamanna stood with both her hands stylishly tucked in the back pocket of her jeans, looking like a vision. She and Sangini struck an immediate rapport. And I began to talk to Sanjay, who revealed himself to be a boastful and pompous man. Unfortunately, Tamanna didn't talk to me much. She, in fact, seemed to be avoiding me while being really nice to Sangini. It perturbed me. But at the same time I felt a certain connection.

On our way home, I kept thinking about her. She had ignited an unmistakable fire in my heart. My rational and logical mind was astonished at these strange tides rising inside me. It was after a very long time that something about myself was surprising me.

That night in bed, I thought about a woman other than Sangini after ages. But my thoughts were accompanied by some guilt. I loved my wife immensely. She had always been the object of my affection and care. But my heart was now on the verge of an unknown and exciting journey. And I could do nothing to hold it back. After fighting the battles of life for years, I had become tired and vulnerable. Tamanna had met me at a very delicate juncture of my life.

Long, intense struggle slowly eats into your stamina, making you exhausted, both physically and mentally. No matter how lively you are, the game of life tests you and tires you. It makes you weak and vulnerable. The same thing happened with me.

Since childhood, I had a habit of leaving things incomplete due to a strange fear of failure. Be it my homework in school or my projects in college, I could never give anything my hundred percent. I always had this severe lack of confidence. As a child, I never knew that this fear, combined with a dearth of good luck, would haunt me in a terrible way for years to come. Apart from these shortcomings, however, I was always disciplined and sincere as a child. I never lied to my teachers and always obeyed my parents. However, during all my school and college years, I could never really figure out as to what I exactly wanted to do. So, after graduation in 1994, when it was time to make a career, I adopted the method of trial and error.

I tried my hands at different businesses—car finance marketing, second hand car sale and purchase, trading in the stock market, to name a few—until my professional graph began to appear like an ECG machine's monitor. All the money I had earned or received from my parents, I lost it either in the stock market or in some very bad business decisions.

For years, I kept fighting with the situation and desperately tried to turn the tables. But every effort went in vain and resulted in yet more losses. Things started going from bad to worse in 2001. Losses resulted in loans and my debts began to mount. Nothing seemed to be working out.

The biggest mistake I made during all these years was not telling my family about my professional life. The fear of shame and insult, combined with a dim and delusional hope of something better coming up, kept me from disclosing the truth. I may have shared it with Sangini but she had a breakdown in 2002 that took four years to heal. Ours was an arranged-cum-love marriage. At that time, I had some money and hoped to make it big using it.

Finally, in 2006, I declared the truth of my professional debacle to my family. The result was, as expected, terrible.

For years, I had been the epitome of sincerity and diligence. I was highly respected by my relatives and my younger cousins looked up to me. Everyone praised what they called my generous and loving heart. Everyone trusted me.

But once I disclosed my reality, I was immediately branded as an undesirable and unsuccessful man. Hearing painful words and facing disturbing situations became a part of my daily routine. My marriage with Sangini hit a rough patch. When we had gotten married, we were both head over heels in love with each other. Sangini had been charmed by my personality, and I had been smitten by her beauty and sincerity. Now, suddenly, our life became a mixture of disharmony and harsh words.

'Ego' was an alien phenomenon to me. Since childhood, I had never shied away from my mistakes. I had always been an ice-breaker, somebody who was always forthcoming. And here also, at such a critical juncture in my life, I accepted my faults and apologised for my mistakes. But nothing stopped the insults and the abuses. All this made me realise that a man might be pardoned a great many faults, but if he is discovered to be a financial failure, he is not easily forgiven.

This backlash could have shattered me, but somewhere deep inside, I was a highly positive man. Despite everything, I had no plans of lying low and crying over my past failures. I was determined to start afresh. I had immense hope, a rock-solid belief that, come what may, things can be changed for the better. With nothing in my hands, I relied on my prayers to give me wisdom and courage. It was as if I was planning to have a rebirth in the same life.

As humans, we are bound to make mistakes and have weaknesses. But once we decide to fight back, everything starts moving in the desired direction. This was my firm belief. And this belief helped me stay calm in the face of all the abuses hurled at me. I decided to fight back and take myself and my family out of the mess I had landed us in.

The reward of all my patience, hard work, and prayers came in 2007, when Babbu, my classmate from school, met me after many years and offered me an educational software project. He was himself struggling in his job as a software engineer and was interested in starting his own venture with me. He had worked painstakingly to develop the project's architecture. I didn't know even the S of software. But I was willing to learn. My responsibility was to persuade schools to use the software and thereby generate business.

Like any start-up, the business was a struggle in the beginning, but we made progress gradually. Soon, along with selling the regular software, we also started making advertising films for our clients. The work made me realise that education and creativity had always been my real passion. After spending three decades of my life wandering aimlessly, I had finally found my calling.

I lost myself in the business. I worked day in and day out. After years of failure, whatever little success we got in the beginning seemed glorious and heady. At the same time, I began writing my first book. The turn of events had unleashed my inner creativity. I had too much bottled up inside and I wanted to vent it all out. A book seemed like the perfect way to do it. I titled it *The Gross Injustice*.

Little did I know that an extraordinary situation was about to knock at the door of my life and change everything forever. It was a delicate period of my life, and I was not expecting any more surprises. But destiny had something else planned for me. It sent Tamanna to me. She came into my rotten life like a breath of freshness and made it seem like everything was possible.

2

Vipin and Pinky invited us to two more get-togethers over the next couple of weekends. Since Tamanna and Sanjay were also invited to these parties, I gladly accepted the invitation both times. The get-togethers were similar to the birthday party, as far as my interaction with Tamanna was concerned. I saw her, admired her, and even though we exchanged only the most necessary of words, I came back from both the parties delighted. Tamanna's thoughts were beginning to overrun my mind. And I had no power to stop the invasion.

A week or two later, the Makhija family moved to the UK. Vipin had got his much awaited job in British Telecom. In hindsight, I feel that the beautiful family had come into our life only to make possible my meeting with Tamanna. Perhaps Tamanna and I were destined to happen.

By that time, we had come close enough to the Sahnis to be able to invite them to our home for drinks and dinner. Our first invitation was accepted readily. And the next two years saw around two dozen get-togethers with just the four of us present. Naturally, we came close as families.

Although seeing and being near Tamanna every now and then was a treat in itself, these get-togethers weren't amazing. And the reason was Sanjay. As Sangini and I got to know him better, we realised that he was a very negative person. He lived on deep-fried food, alcohol, and cigarettes, was a self-proclaimed genius (although in every sense he looked and sounded like an average Joe), and dominated all conversations. He was highly self-obsessed and arrogant. For him, friendship meant going out, eating and drinking, and mocking others.

In his presence, Tamanna didn't talk much, and whatever little she spoke was generally with Sangini. However, whenever she did speak, she talked sense, unlike her husband. Her observations were highly intelligent. She was sweet, smart, well-spoken, polite, sensitive, and overall an amazing person. She was a combination of beauty and brains. For me, this was her biggest sex appeal.

However, because of her pompous husband, we both barely talked, barely made eye contact. Most of the times, she even avoided greeting me. She was always on the guard when we met. And that "guard" was sometimes disturbing. I would wonder, *Why doesn't she talk to me?* It would upset me for hours, but never long enough to stop me from continuing to fall in love with her, deeper and deeper.

Within two months of meeting her, the irrational part of my mind began to dominate my daytime thoughts.

One morning I was in the bathroom, brushing my teeth, when suddenly a thought popped up in my mind. *Tamanna must be doing the same thing as well.*

Gosh! That was ridiculous. From where did Tamanna appear at 7:30 a.m. in my bathroom?

Another day, I was eating my breakfast, a cheese sandwich, and a similar thought emerged in my mind. *Tamanna must be fond of cheese sandwich too. She must be having her breakfast at this very moment as well.*

Similar thoughts kept cropping up in my mind every now and then. *Tamanna must be bathing too. Tamanna must be sweating too. Tamanna must be walking on the streets too. Tamanna must be watching this TV show too.*

Tamanna must like this, must like that. Tamanna must be doing this, she must be doing that.

Good God! What was I thinking? Was I out of my senses?

I was shocked to find such thoughts in my mind. Tamanna and I had barely interacted. I didn't know her very well. What was happening to me? My marriage, my daughter, and my business were my reality. There was already an abundance of struggles and tensions in my life. Then what was I doing?

Tamanna had a family too. I was sure all my feelings for her were one-sided. Yet I would keep thinking about her.

Love happens—with whom, how and when? No one can predict. All through my life, I had made fun of romantic movies and of all those people who declared they were in love. While making fun of romantic films, and their heroes and heroines, I used to say that movies distort youngsters' minds, that they show a world of make-believe. I used to laugh at all the silly, romantic, mushy stuff they showed.

But now, the same thing was happening to me. True, I had fallen in love before—with Sangini—but that had never been like this. With Sangini, it was a gradual process. We both had freely allowed ourselves to grow close to each other. With Tamanna, in contrast, it was entirely mysterious. I had not expected to fall in love with her, let alone planned it. Our match was forbidden and, therefore, had a tinge of excitement to it. It was not the love of grown-ups, it was the madness of teenage.

And most importantly, it was love that could not be controlled.

By the beginning of 2008, Tamanna was in my thoughts

throughout the day, from morning till evening and even at night. She was in every nook and corner of my head. I was virtually eating with her, drinking with her, going out with her, coming home with her, sleeping with her, waking up with her.

We met with the Sahnis often. Many times we went for family outings as well. Tamanna had a nice way of walking. I would involuntarily watch her getting out of the car and my mind would echo just one thing: *Oh I love her!*

What are you saying, Arjun? Have you gone crazy? Pat, the second echo would resound in my mind.

***

Keeping my feelings for Tamanna only to myself wasn't easy. I couldn't have kept such a heavy baggage of thoughts undisclosed from the outside world forever. After all, we all need to unload our emotions, share our dreams and desires with someone. After keeping the gates of my secret closed for about fifteen months, I opened them in June, 2008. I told Babbu about my hopeless situation.

Babbu's real name was Mrityunjay. I'd found it a tongue twister ever since school and had very conveniently opted for his nickname, Babbu, like the rest of the class. The nickname suited him better too, because Babbu looked and behaved every bit like a "Babbu." He was a dusky, five-feet-eleven-inch tall, heavily built man, with a protruding belly that boasted of numerous beer bottles. He was the closest anyone had come to being my best friend. We both had been through extreme rough patches in our personal and professional lives and so were very close.

One day, when we were both alone and free in office, I confided in him, "Something strange is happening to me."

I told him everything.

It took me almost an hour to explain what I was going through. He listened to me ardently and patiently, which was quite unlike him. After I had finished, he turned to gaze at the sky through the window of our cabin, with the slightest hint of a smile on his face.

Will he make fun of me? I wondered. After waiting for a couple of seconds, I finally asked, "Do you have anything to say?"

Still smiling, Babbu turned his gaze back to me. Then, he got up from his chair and walked around the table towards me. "*Haan, yaar,*" he said and placed his hand on my shoulder, "I have understood everything." His tone was compassionate.

At least there is someone who understands my feelings, I exulted.

"I know what has to be done now," Babbu continued, looking directly into my eyes. "You need to have a session of decent sex, my friend."

That was what he had concluded!

"I didn't expect this from you," I said.

"No, I am serious," he said.

"Shut up, man!" I shouted.

"Dude, I am not kidding," he said. "This is happening because you are under so much pressure. Extreme tension often results in such situations. You have no respect, no peace at home, work is hard, and there is nothing to fall back upon. You need rest, you need complete relaxation. Don't worry. I'll do something for you."

"What? What'll you do?" I asked, wondering what he'd meant by that offer.

"Well, it's simple, very simple. I'll speak to someone. Will try to arrange someone for you."

This was my friend Babbu, who had claimed to have understood my problem.

I sighed. "Stop using your useless brain. You know I have never done such a cheap thing in my life. And I'll never do it either. This is not a funny situation. I expected some amount of decency from you."

"What is indecent about this?" he shot back. "Look, it's okay. You're thirty-six, and things with Sangini Bhabhi are not going very well. These things are bound to happen! Tell me, has she given any indications to you?"

"No!"

Babbu smiled. "See, I knew it! It's very simple: you need someone in your life. You need a good stormy session of passionate sex. And you need it on a regular basis. Trust me, you will be okay after that."

I stared at him in despair. "Thank you very much. Your advice was very valuable."

Babbu laughed. "Oh come on, don't take me otherwise. In your circumstances, you are bound to get attracted to any woman you come across."

"But I haven't gotten attracted to anyone ever since I got married to Sangini. There were times when I could have had my pick, but I never went that way. I have been in worse situations, but it was always only Sangini for me. Always."

"Hmmm," he sighed. "I know you since school, Arjun. You always used to make fun of romantic movies and all such stuff. You always called your relationship as mature romance. But now, nine years into your marriage, with a family by your side, you are seeing a moron's wife in the cheese sandwich you are eating?"

We both started laughing. Babbu had met Sanjay at a get-together at my place. Later, we both had made fun of him.

"This calls for a party," Babbu resumed after he'd laughed to his heart's content. "At eighteen you made fun of love and acted over-mature. Now, at thirty-six, you are behaving like a teenager in love. That's the game of time, my friend."

That was true. I shook my head, smiling. After having shared everything with someone and not being judged for it, I was feeling very light. It was as if a huge burden had been lifted off my shoulders. I realised that Babbu was the kind of friend who would always trust me, no matter what I was doing. I was immensely grateful to him for this.

But, on a more sensible note, he was a jerk! For the next half an hour, he frantically searched Facebook and Orkut for the new girl in his friend's life, but in vain. Tamanna was nowhere.

"Stop it!" I was becoming somewhat irritated.

"Oh come on, I have the right to find my bhabhiji."

Both of us burst into laughter again. God bless such friends.

3

I had three girls in my social circle. One was a neighbour, while the other two I knew from work. All of them were in their mid-twenties and were pretty and attractive. I had great affection for all of them and shared a dignified relationship with each.

One day, towards the end of 2008, Sneha, one of the two girls I knew from work, called me up. She sounded disturbed. When I enquired, she told me she was facing some strange problem in her career. She wanted to meet me and discuss it. I immediately planned a meeting at a nearby CCD the next day.

We discussed her troubles over coffee and sandwiches. They were indeed strange. She told me story after story of how something awful happened wherever she started working. Either the department she joined would be closed down a few weeks after she joined or the whole company would shut shop. Sometimes, the office would prove to be severely unprofessional, and sometimes very unproductive. After quitting job after job, she had become convinced that something was wrong with her, that some evil spirit was upon her, that her career was jinxed, something like that. She had called me after learning that the company she was currently working in was considering shutting down her division. The news had depressed her and she had stopped going to work. She was emotionally weak and held my hand in hers the entire time we were there. She was crying and needed support.

I told her to stop being superstitious and have faith in God. I advised her to remain optimistic and rational and strong. Something decent and lasting was sure to turn up sooner or later. I gave her my example and told her how I had found my destination and my calling after struggling for more than ten years.

When we stepped out of the cafe, she hugged me tightly and looked at me longingly. She thanked me for listening to her and giving her time out of my busy routine. I asked her to call me if she wanted to share anything else and said goodbye.

On my way home, I felt very proud of myself. I congratulated myself on handling the situation very well. Maybe it was the wisdom attained in the last ten years of my life that had made me act so maturely. Most men would have tried to take advantage of the vulnerable and superstitious girl, but I had done nothing of that sort. Instead, I had given her the right advice. She had held my hand, hugged me, looked at me longingly, but I had not even felt like doing anything wrong. I just wanted her to be happy and to regain her lost confidence. I just wanted to be there for her.

She called me many times in the next fifteen days. Each time, she would ask to meet me somewhere on some pretext or the other. But not once did I succumb to the temptation. I told her firmly to look after her career. I gave her a lot of pep talk and counselled her continuously.

Then, finally, more than two weeks after our CCD meeting, she rejoined her office. A few days later, she called me to request a meeting. She wanted to thank me personally. This time, she sounded happy, so I said yes.

We met that weekend, this time at a Barista nearby. When I met her, I could see happiness in her entire being: her eyes, her body language, her lips, everything seemed to be smiling. She observed me quietly as I added sugar to my coffee. When I looked up, I found her beaming at me. She leaned forward and held my hand.

"Thank you, Arjun," she whispered. "Your support and advice really helped me. I had lost my way." She paused. "My parents struggled really hard to educate me. And I have immense pressure to become financially successful and make them proud. All the pressure and bad luck had broken my spirit, but you pieced it back together. Thank you." Tears trickled down her cheeks. I squeezed her hand reassuringly. "I am a young girl," she continued. "I have emotions. I was vulnerable. But you didn't take advantage of me. If you had not acted maturely, we would have ended up doing something stupid for sure."

I smiled, more proud of myself than I'd ever been before.

We continued talking about her career and life for a long time. She had only one educational degree: a Mass Com from JNU. So I advised her to study more to give a boost to her career and her salary in the current job. She agreed instantly. She had always wanted to do an MBA in International Trade and decided to look for colleges from where she could study that without having to quit her job. When we moved out of Barista, she again embraced me. This time, it was a friendly embrace, one filled with gratitude.

I remained in touch with Sneha for many years. That company she worked for never shut down her division. She also got an MBA from IGNOU. She remained grateful to me for helping her during that tough period in her life.

As already mentioned, this episode made me very proud of myself. I realised I had evolved a lot as a person when I was struggling with my life. But the incident made me realise something more, something worrisome. My meeting and counselling with Sneha proved that my love for Tamanna was not based on lust and sexual frustration, as Babbu had suspected. I could have easily slept with Sneha, but that thought had never crossed my mind. This meant that I had truly fallen for Tamanna. My feelings for her were true, pure, and strong.

***

We had expanded our business from Delhi to Chandigarh. Yet, things were not going very smoothly. Establishing our new business was far tougher a task than what Babbu and I had imagined. Even after more than a year of hard work, we were finding it difficult to generate enough revenue. We barely managed to pay our staff their salaries. Our profits were minimal.

In India, convincing people to pay money for the beneficial services that they use is the most difficult task. We faced a similar situation. Our project was a revolutionary one and was very thoughtfully designed. But at the time of presenting the financial implications, the client would show his sheer inability and helplessness in implementing it in his/her institution.

Reason? Severe lack of finances! People who owned luxury cars worth 25 lacs would quote ridiculous excuses like this.

We had some good-paying clients too, but they were only a handful. So, in spite of extending our work base to a wider area, finances were a constraint.

Whatever the situation might be, Tamanna remained inside me. I would often secretly talk to her in my thoughts. Sometimes I would tell her about some complicated professional challenge, sometimes I would complain how tired I was.

Entering home at the end of each day had become most difficult. When there were no fights, an uncomfortable silence lingered in the house, threatening to explode.

Even though my relationship with Sangini had become really tense and weak, not even once did I blame her for the anger she would often show towards me, for the heart-piercing words that would so often greet me. A good financial position is the key to survival in this practical world, and she had not seen enough money in the last so many years.

There was just one silver lining: I had finished writing my book and had even found a publisher for it. It was a reputable publishing house. My friend had introduced me to its director. My book was slated to be out in the first half of 2009.

Meanwhile, I continued to share my problems with Babbu. Apart from my discords with Sangini, I would also tell him, at least ten times a day, that I was in love with Tamanna.

"Are you going crazy?" Babbu asked one day, serious.

"This is impossible. This is risky. This is suicidal!" he exclaimed another day.

"You have no future with her. This relationship is impossible," he tried counselling a week after that.

When I told him about Sneha, he was shocked. "Are you nuts? You desperately needed relief in life, and see what you did. You sucker, vermin, asshole! I think you need a psychiatrist."

The next day, he came to my desk, looking grave. "Listen, Arjun." He hesitated. "Have you gone impotent?"

God! I burst into laughter. After I assured him that there was no such problem with me, he said, "I have started getting worried for you, *yaar*!"

At the end of the day, on our way towards the parking lot, he said, "I fully understand your situation, but you are not letting me help you."

"Thanks, man, but no thanks," I replied as we got into his car.

"Everything is for pleasure, man! Don't try to fool me or yourself. These affairs are for sex and there's no harm in having sex outside! I say it is absolutely correct."

That's dirty, that is cheating!" I objected.

"No", Arjun, no! There is nothing wrong in having sex outside. See, you are having only sex and nothing more! No commitment and no involvement, nothing! And when there is no involvement, then how does the question of 'cheating' arise?"

***

One day in January 2009, I was travelling back home in an auto. Usually, either Babbu drove me to our Janakpuri office in his car or I drove him in my car, but that day Babbu hadn't come to work and my car's tyre was punctured. Unwilling to waste time in changing the tyre, I had taken an auto in the morning, and was now returning home in another.

Cruel, cold winds hit me relentlessly as the auto hurtled its way across south-west Delhi. Despite being covered in layers of warm clothes, I shivered. But I didn't mind it so much because, as usual, I was thinking about Tamanna. Lately, our family get-togethers had become very difficult for me. It took me all my energy to refrain from speaking to her. When she was at home, all my concentration would be on her. I would sit in the room, tense and watchful, not paying much attention to anything else. Though Tamanna's attitude towards me was still largely cold and distant, she had said words of appreciation for me a couple of times. Once, she had proclaimed that I was the first sincere friend of her husband. Another time, she had indirectly called me good-hearted and a nice person. Saying that, she had smiled. Her sparkling white teeth made her smile even more beautiful.

"Your smile is happiness for me, Tamanna!" my mind had loudly echoed.

I was beginning to get increasingly scared that I might actually utter something stupid someday. So far, I had convincingly managed to hide my emotions from everyone. In this, my theatre experience from school had helped me. Performing arts had been my passion at that time and now it was helping me conceal the storm that constantly raged in my head.

Suddenly, the auto began to jerk, and finally, it came to a halt. I was very much aware of where we were. We were in the Tagore Garden locality where Tamanna's house was. I always took the main road to reach my house. But the auto driver had taken a short cut that passed by the Sahnis' house. The auto in fact had halted only a couple of yards from it. I could see a woman standing in front of it, buying something from a *chaat*wallah. Today was my lucky day!

Under normal circumstances, I would have waited for the autowallah to see what the problem with the auto was. If it was something serious, I would have given him a reduced fare. But that day, I quickly but quietly got down from the vehicle and paid the man the full fare. Then I turned and continued on my way, on foot. My pulse quickened as I neared the hawker's cart. The woman was indeed Tamanna, I could now see her clearly. Only a while back, I was shivering in the auto. Now I was sweating. My heart was pounding inside my chest.

This was the first time I would meet Tamanna alone, without Sanjay around. Nobody could stop that now. This was my moment.

"*Bhaisaab*, you forgot your tiffin!" the auto driver shouted from behind. IDIOT! Why the fuck did he have to shout? I turned back and quietly took my tiffin box from him. But it was useless. Tamanna was already looking in my direction. I rushed forward.

"Arjun?" she asked, surprised, when she recognised me. "What are you doing here? What happened?"

I was completely blank, lost. I stood there awkwardly, staring at her. Her beautiful face was lit up by the streetlight above us. Behind me, the autowallah started his vehicle. The loud noise brought me back to reality. "*Arey*, this thing broke down," I said, trying to sound casual. "How are you?"

"I am good," she said, smiling. "But you look a little disturbed. Is everything okay?"

Shit! "Yes, yes, everything's okay." I pulled out my handkerchief and started wiping the sweat off my face. "So, you're buying *tikkies*?" I tried to change the topic.

She nodded. "Vicky loves them," she said. Her observant eyes were carefully scanning my face. "Arjun, you look tense," she remarked again. "You sure everything's okay?"

No, I'm not sure. I am married and have a lovely family, but I keep thinking about you the whole day, damn it. I am the moron who has fallen in love with his friend's wife. On top of that, my business is not going very well. We can't seem to generate enough money despite all our efforts. My wife fights with me every other day, and my family doesn't like me anymore. So yeah, nothing's okay, all right? Nothing's okay!

Obviously I couldn't say all that, that too in the middle of the road. So I casually replied, "All is well, Tamanna. Just everyday stresses."

"When are you coming out with your book?" came the second question. "I am eager to read it."

I promise you'll get the first copy, my mind echoed. "It'll be out soon," I said.

She smiled softly and nodded. There was something on her mind. With Sanjay absent, she seemed more forthcoming than usual.

"I am looking forward to it. I'm sure it will be a bestseller. I will pray for it."

I was on cloud nine. "Thank you, thank you so much. That's very sweet of you."

She laughed. "Okay, I must get back inside. Vicky must be waiting for his *tikkies*. Hey, why don't you join us?"

"No, no, Sangini must be waiting. I must go," I declined the invitation. I'd have given anything to be able to spend more time with her but I knew Sanjay would be inside (I could see his car parked across the road) and I didn't want to meet him.

"Oh, yes, of course," she said, and picked up her order. "Bye then, take care." She turned around and started walking towards her home. When she was at the door, she turned back and saw me staring at her. Embarrassed, I looked down and took out my phone.

She smiled. "No matter how much you hide it, Arjun, I know there's something bothering you. You don't look okay. Your eyes are saying it all. I don't know what it is, but I know something else—you are a nice person and things will surely become better for you." Then, without waiting for my response, she disappeared behind the door.

I was stunned. Not only had the woman I loved noticed I was disturbed, she had also called me a nice person. She had said she'd pray for my book and assured me that things will become all right. At that moment, I didn't care whether things were going to become better or not. All that mattered was that Tamanna had confidence in me and she thought I was a nice person.

I was happy. I was very happy. I was really very happy.

Tamanna had noticed my anguish! I mattered to her! She cared for me! Does she . . .? Was she . . . really? I wondered.

In his beautiful novel *The Alchemist*, Paulo Coelho says, "And, when you want something, all the universe conspires in helping you to achieve it." Shah Rukh Khan's *Om Shanti Om* had a similar line: "*Agar kisi cheez ko dil se chaaho to puri kayanat usey tumse milane ki koshish mein lag jaati hai.*"

For the past many months, each time I had missed, *really* missed Tamanna, an uncontrollable desire would shoot out of my soul into the universe for her. That night, it felt like somebody up there had finally listened to my desires.

Babbu's sickness, my car's puncture, the auto, the *chaat*wallah . . . it seemed like the universe had conspired to make possible that meeting between Tamanna and me.

4

As soon as I had a minute the next morning, I dialled Babbu's number to tell him about my meeting with Tamanna. My mind was filled with too many thoughts and speculations and I just had to share the news with someone. I was going crazy with excitement and happiness. Unfortunately, Babbu's number was "not reachable." *Fucker!*

I couldn't wait till I reached office to share everything with him. I wasn't even sure whether he would be coming to office that day. So I decided to call my other best friend, Happy. Happy and I were childhood friends. We lived in the same locality. Like Babbu, he was appropriately named. He was a happy-go-lucky man who believed in spreading smiles and laughter. Though he was five years elder to me, he looked ten years younger. He used to be a professional cricket player and looked like it. He had played junior county cricket in England for twelve years. After retiring from the game in 2002, he had returned to India and his old home. After that, our bond of friendship had strengthened even further.

I dialled Happy's number, but the sucker's phone was switched off.

Double whammy! Gosh, I have the best friends in the world!

I stood on the spot for some time, cursing my friends. Then an idea struck me.

I had inherited a huge collection of music from my father, who was a connoisseur of famous records. For most of my life, I had ignored this valuable inheritance because after graduation, I had more or less stopped listening to music. There was so much to do and worry about—where did one have the time to listen to singers sing about pain, love, and passion?

But that day, I had a craving to see all the cassettes and CDs. I ran to my room, opened the storage box of my double bed, and pulled out some bags.

"What the hell are you doing, Arjun?" Sangini asked when she saw me. She looked baffled and suspicious. But who could blame her? After all, her husband was looking through bags that hadn't been opened in more than a decade.

I pulled out the audio cassette of Shah Rukh's *Darr*. "I was looking for this," I said.

"What do you want to do with this old cassette?"

"Well . . ." I tried to think of a convincing answer. Why did I want *Darr*'s cassette? "Babbu wants it." Friends always come handy in such situations.

"Your friends are like you only," she commented and left the room.

I played the cassette on my way to work. And would you believe it, it played perfectly! I thanked the recording company.

On the road, with the music playing loud, I felt like I was flying. Nothing bothered me, not even Delhi's maddening traffic. I could see Tamanna everywhere, her innocent eyes looking into mine. The air was full of her fragrance. She had said I was a nice person. She was going to pray for my book. I sang along with Udit Narayan.

Mere khaabo ki tasveer hai tu,
Bekhabar, meri taqdeer hai tu . . .

Gosh! ARJUN, WHAT ARE YOU DOING?

Crashing, I came back to reality, back to my senses. I scolded myself and concentrated on the driving. The traffic began to bother me. Everything smelled of dust, pollution, and heat. I cursed other drivers and sped my way to the office. Suddenly, Tamanna was lost . . . but not for long.

When I parked my car near my office and got down, my gaze fell upon a huge poster of Deepika Padukone. It was an advertisement of a leading cosmetic brand and was hung over the side of the Satyam Cineplex building.

She looks so like Tamanna. So beautiful! This was my first thought. I was surprised. It was the first time I was noticing the close resemblance between Deepika and Tamanna. I kept staring at the poster for a couple of minutes. My heart was soaring again. Now I had two things to tell Babbu about.

Excited, I made my way towards the office. I found Babbu busy on his laptop, looking somewhat irritated.

"Hi," I said.

In response, Babbu only nodded. He didn't even look up at me. This was unusual.

"Hey, I have something to share," I tried again.

"Hmm," he replied. "Wait."

I was running out of patience. I walked to his side of the table to see what he was so busy with.

Simmi—his browser window was full of different tabs with that name. I was surprised. Who was Simmi? There used to be a girl with the same name in our school . . .

"What are you doing?" I enquired.

He didn't reply. Something was fishy. Babbu never acted like this.

"Who is Simmi?" I asked again.

A smile broke on Babbu's lips. He was blushing!

"Is this the same Simmi we knew in school?" I demanded.

"Uh, well, actually . . . yes, she's the same girl," Babbu replied. He sounded somewhat embarrassed. By now, I was intrigued. Babbu seemed to have a big secret.

"Why are you looking for her today?"

Babbu chuckled and blushed even more. "Actually, there's something that you don't know," he replied. "But please don't keep standing here on my head like this. Sit and I will explain everything."

I wasted no time in running to my chair. Once seated, I ordered Babbu, "Okay, out with it."

"You remember we all were friends in school?" It seemed as if Babbu had to make a tremendous effort just to speak.

I nodded.

"So, umm, she, I mean, this Simmi used to come to Vikram's house. You remember that?"

I nodded again, impatiently.

"You know she was Vikram's *rakhi* sister?"

"Yes! So what, sucker? I remember everything. Come to the point! Why now? Why today!"

"Yes, yes, wait! Actually, in those days I noticed she liked me," Babbu finally revealed. He was such a jerk! I never knew about this.

"All these years you hid it from me? Great, that was very well done! You are a great friend!"

"You were a very good friend of Vikram. I felt a little awkward in revealing the truth."

I nodded. But he still hadn't answered why he was searching for her today after sixteen long years. Was he still in touch with her? No, he wasn't, otherwise why would he be searching for her?

"Actually, she liked me a lot," Babbu continued. "And you know how we were in those days . . . just ready to blast."

"Blast" meant "always horny."

"So then?" I pushed him to say more.

Babbu laughed. "Well, she was Vikram's *rakhi* sister, so I had to control myself."

"Did she ever say anything to you?" I asked.

"Umm, well, it was all indirect," he answered. "I could see it in her behaviour and in her eyes!"

I was now getting irritated. He wasn't revealing the full thing and I could sense that.

"So? Then? Why now! Why today!" I almost shouted.

"Don't get hyper, *yaar*. I am telling you everything."

I wanted to hit him then and there, but I couldn't. I was really curious to know the full story. So I clenched my teeth and nodded.

"In the final days of school, she started calling on my phone by some other name," Babbu resumed. "I knew it was her. She was desperate for me. And before the final Economics board exam, she said something . . ."

Oh boy! "You scored badly in economics, I remember that. You were the best in the whole section, everybody expected you to score ninety, but you got what? Sixty-five?"

"Forty-nine."

It was because of his score in Economics that Babbu had failed to get admission in the college of his choice. In the end, he had had to compromise and settle for a B-grade college. What had Simmi told him that he performed so poorly? I was dying to know.

"So, what did she say to you that day?"

"We had become very good phone friends by then, but somehow she always sounded desperate. She—"

"What did she say, MORON? Tell me now!" I shouted.

"'Will you fuck me, Babbu?'" He finally dropped the bombshell.

"Whaaaaaaaat?" My mouth was wide open in disbelief. This was the mother of all secrets. "No, that can't be true!"

Babbu didn't respond. He just sat there, expressionless. For the next few seconds, there was complete silence in the room. We were both lost in our thoughts. He was my very good friend, but had he ever been able to impress a girl? I had serious doubts about that.

"And then? After that, what?" I finally broke the silence.

"Nothing after that, *yaar*! I don't know what happened to me, but I got nervous, really nervous. You know I was already involved with Sonia."

"Nooooooooooooo!" I couldn't believe it.

"Seriously, *yaar*. From that day I stopped talking to her."

"That's unbelievable, man!"

"The whole night I kept dreaming about her. 'Will you fuck me, Babbu?' Her voice kept ringing in my ears. I couldn't study at all."

I could almost imagine the kind of dreams he must have had that night. I also felt bad for him. The fucker had lost his chance to study at a good college for nothing.

"That was really unfortunate, *yaar*," I sympathised.

Babbu nodded dejectedly. "Yeah, man, that was an open invitation. She was desperate. She would've been surely terrific inside."

Great! I was expressing my consolation for his Economics tragedy, and he thought that I was feeling bad for his missed chance of having sex with Simmi! All this still hadn't answered the important question.

"Why are you googling her today? God knows where she

might be. Must be married, with children. Sixteen years is a pretty long period."

At that, Babbu leaned back in his chair and sighed. "You are responsible for this," he said

"Me? What do you mean?"

"Your passion for Tamanna got my feelings ignited too."

"That's ridiculous." I laughed at him. "Our situations are very different. My feelings for Tamanna are pure and platonic, and yours—"

"And mine are for sex? Pure sex? Right?" He sounded angry.

"It appears so!" I said. "Isn't this cheating on your wife?"

"Aren't you doing the same?" he promptly replied.

"How come?" Now, I was angry.

"It doesn't matter which road you take to reach the brothel."

"Shut up! What kind of an example is that?" I protested.

"Okay, okay! Let's change it to cinema hall, all right? So, does it matter which route you take?"

I had no immediate answer to that. Babbu looked at me for some response, which didn't come. So he continued.

"Don't take me otherwise. You have every right to think about Tamanna. I respect your feelings for her. In fact, I'm ready to help you in every way possible to get her. I don't want you to have any regrets in the future."

I smiled.

"One should not have any regrets. And Simmi is my regret, *yaar*. A big regret. Even after school, I had many girlfriends in college, but that Simmi . . . uff!" He sighed. "I never forgot her. Later, by the time I thought of talking to her, she had changed her house and her telephone number. I have seen so many girls, but none was as desperate as she was. Nobody has ever said such a thing to me. 'Will you fuck me, Babbu?'"

For the next two minutes, we were in a fit of laughter. Our situation was tragic but hilarious. At thirty-six, we were talking like sixteen-year-olds.

When Babbu caught his breath, he said, "Listen, you are in touch with Amit, na? He used to be Simmi's neighbour. Will you call him up and see if he can give any information on Simmi?"

"Wait, is this why you have been supporting my love for Tamanna? So that I will help you with this?"

Babbu smiled mischievously. "Shut up, *yaar*, and just call Amit."

I gave him a stern look and called up Amit, but he didn't take my call. After five attempts, he sent me a message saying that he was out of Delhi and would surely call me back the next day.

That made Babbu hopeful and happy. So I told him about Deepika Padukone's poster and my meeting with Tamanna.

"Wow, man, love is in the air!" he said. "Keep it up. I am totally with you!"

That made my day. I was grateful for his support. But little did I know that Babbu's attitude would change the next day after Amit's call.

I told Amit clearly about why I was looking for Simmi. He listened to everything very attentively. And then, he started laughing hysterically.

"You jerks!" he said. "You haven't changed even a single bit in the last so many years. Good, *yaar*, the fire is still burning inside you two."

Then he told me that Simmi and her family had left his neighbourhood many years ago and he had no clue about their current location. He promised to ask around and help us trace her. He said he'd call in a while.

True to his word, he called us in the evening. But he had

bad news. He said he couldn't get any information about Simmi. Babbu was disheartened and very angry, so much so that when I pointed at Deepika's poster later when we were talking towards his car, he reprimanded me, "Fuck you, man. Now you have started seeing her in posters. This is not love but frustration of life."

5

Ten days after my chance meeting with Tamanna, the Sahnis came to our place for drinks and dinner. After serving them *papad* and peanuts, Sangini and I sat down with them with a bottle of Tuborg and glasses. As Sangini started pouring everyone a chilled glass of beer, Sanjay started telling us a story he had narrated dozens of times before. I looked up at Tamanna and found her rolling her eyes. Clearly, she was as irritated by Sanjay's stale old stories as we were. She was wearing a pink sleeveless kurta with black jeans. Her eyes were kohled and her hair was tied up in a loose bun. As usual, she looked sophisticated and pretty.

Sanjay loved to talk about himself and his achievements. Not only was he shamelessly boastful, he was also rude and ill-mannered. All he talked about was his previous jobs and how he had excelled at them. According to him, he had worked in all the top-notch companies of India. But all this seemed highly debatable and doubtful to me. At the time, he was managing a primary school started by his parents. He had had an accident some years ago, after which he had been in coma for about two months. After that . . . what? I'm not sure. Frankly, I could never really connect the distorted fragments of claims that he was always making. I could not even make out the exact time frame of his accident.

I could never discuss my personal problems with him. Neither would he ever share anything with me. That sort of conversation was just not his cup of tea. Once, I attempted to tell him about my financial struggles. He interrupted me midway and replied in a rather insulting tone, "Dude, if you work like a jerk, you're bound to end up a failure." The only reason I continued my friendship with him after that day was because he was Tamanna's husband.

That day, after Sanjay had finished his boring story, the discussion somehow reached the Bill Clinton-Monica Lewinsky affair. There, Tamanna made a connection with the charismatic American president J.F. Kennedy, and I brought in the Cuban Missile Crisis of the early 1960s. Sanjay's role in the conversation was only till the Bill-Monica affair. He apparently didn't know anything about either JFK or Cuba.

"Didn't the Crisis happen during Kennedy's term?" I was saying. "After he became the president in 1962—"

"Excuse me, Arjun," Tamanna interrupted me. "Kennedy became president in 1961, not '62. And even though the Crisis happened during his term, its seeds had been sown in the time of Eisenhower, the thirty-fourth president of America. The October 1962 confrontation between the Soviet Union, Cuba, and the United States was the result of tensions that had been building for years."

Oh boy! Oh my lord! I was floored. Who would not want a wife as smart as Tamanna? She was truly an incredible combination of beauty and brains. For some moments, I lost my guard.

"Yes, Tamanna, you're right!" I put my hand over hers. "Thank you for correcting me. How do you remember all these details?"

Tamanna was embarrassed. She was blushing. In that

moment, she looked more beautiful than Aishwarya Rai.

Suddenly, I realised the presence of the other two people in the room. I pulled my hand away. Sangini, as simple as ever, was smiling at us. But Sanjay did not look too happy. There was an awkward silence, which Tamanna quickly broke.

"It's nothing really, Arjun. I had read this back in school in a general affairs book. And somehow I never forgot it."

"You are being modest," Sangini said.

Sanjay changed the topic, and I went inside to get some more beer. That was the first time I had touched Tamanna. I had never planned it. It just happened—it was a spontaneous action, coming from my heart. Her hands had been a little moist. Carefully, I looked around, and, on finding no one, I closed my fists and slowly rubbed my palm, trying to secure her sweat inside me. A portion of Tamanna had come to me today. I was feeling deliriously happy.

I went back to the living room to find Tamanna and Sangini discussing their weekend plans. Sanjay was busy with his mobile. I refreshed everyone's beer, sat down at my place, and slowly opened my palm. It was now moist with our sweat. Yeah, it was ours now!

"Hey, what are you humming?" Tamanna said after a couple of minutes. It was then that I realised that I had been humming a tune. Such was the effect of Tamanna's presence on me. "Why don't you sing for everyone? Sangini has told me you have a beautiful voice."

I said no initially, but when everyone insisted, I had to say okay. I cleared my throat. My heartbeat quickened. This was going to be the first time that I'd sing in front of Tamanna.

How can I tell her I don't miss her whenever I am away?
How can I say it's you I think of every single night and day?

I had barely started when I blanked out and stopped.

"That was wonderful, Arjun. Go on!" Tamanna urged.

"I forgot the lyrics!" I said.

"Which song is this? You have never sung it before," Sangini commented.

"This is a very old song. Wait, I know it," Tamanna said. "Umm, Lobo? Right?"

I nodded, even more impressed. She had a great knowledge of music too. Her intelligent mind, her sex appeal, was making me weaker and weaker. To hell with the guard! I had to respond, now!

I was about to say something—I don't remember what, but something stupid for sure—when Sanjay asked his wife, "How do *you* know this song?"

Very smartly, Tamanna just smiled in response.

"You are a lucky man, Sanjay," I turned to Sanjay and said.

Sanjay made a funny face at that, like he couldn't care less.

Tamanna said, "Sangini is luckier. She told me all about how you took care of her during her rough phase."

"Rough phase? I don't know about this," Sanjay said. "Tell me the story."

For the next fifteen minutes, Tamanna told her husband about Sangini's nervous breakdown of 2002.

Sangini had lost her father at a young age, just like I had. Her father had died in a road accident and the trauma had scarred her very deeply. She often had nightmares about blood and death and was always fearful of the unknown. When our daughter was born, her paranoia increased. She was constantly terrified that something bad might happen to her.

Soon, she had a mental breakdown. She became obsessive about cleanliness. She would spend many hours cleaning just a couple of utensils in the kitchen. She would keep brushing her teeth for more than fifteen minutes. She would wake up in the middle of the night, crying bitterly. Many times, even during the day, she would break down for no reason at all.

I found myself alone with her at the time. None of our relatives helped us. The Indian society doesn't understand psychological problems. Sangini was dismissed as "mad" and a "mental case." I got a lot of sympathy but no support. Only my mother and Sangini's mother were with us, but even they could not do much. I had to take control of our life and help Sangini. It was a really difficult time. My career was already an enormous source of worry for me. On top of that, Sangini's health had worsened too.

I took Sangini to doctors and psychologists. We even tried Reiki. I personally counselled her as well. I told her about Buddhist meditation and that worked wonders. After four years of hard work, I finally brought her back on track. When I look back today on those times, I have mixed feelings. I was successful at times and a failure at others. Some of my advice helped Sangini, but some was harmful too. But through those terrible storms, I never let go of Sangini's hand, and I am proud of myself for that. At that time I had made a commitment to myself, of being her friend, companion, brother, sister, father, and soul mate. This attitude of mine was in no way an obligation to her. She was every bit worth it. She was a gem—a big-hearted, dutiful, wonderful person.

After she finished her narration, Tamanna turned to me and said, "You did very well, Arjun. God bless you."

There was a wide smile on my face. This was the first time I was hearing what Sangini thought of the role I played in her recovery. I had not known that she had narrated the story to Tamanna in such great detail. I was surprised and delighted. My heart filled with affection and gratitude for my wife. I was also glad to know that due to this story, I had probably entered into Tamanna's good books.

***

On the following Monday, I shared everything with Babbu, as excited as a sixteen-year-old after his first kiss. But Babbu's mood was off. He had not been able to track Simmi down. Even I had used all my contacts and called all our old batchmates in order to reach Simmi. But to no avail. Simmi was not in touch with anyone. So Babbu responded to my updates without any excitement.

So I soaked in my divine emotions of love all by myself for the whole week. Babbu's mood did not improve and I stopped sharing things with him. Therefore, Friday found me thinking about Happy, my other best friend. Happy was the frankest and craziest person I knew. He had interesting things to say about everything. For instance, according to him, "Farting is a very democratic way of expression."

One day he told me how very mad his girlfriend was at him. When I asked him the reason, he said, "She called from Spain to talk to me, but I didn't attend the call."

"Why? Why didn't you take the call?" I asked.

"I was jacking off to a blue film in the drawing room. The scenes were too good, man! When I told her this, she got mad."

This is how honest Happy was. I realised it was high time I told him about my love for Tamanna and see what he had to say. It was the perfect time too—Friday evening. We could chill over beer and talk nonsense. I called him up, only to learn that he had a terribly upset stomach. So instead of beer, I had to take apple juice to his place.

"What's up, man?" I asked when I saw him. He was lying

in bed, looking very weak. "You must've eaten something wrong."

"I don't know, man," replied Happy. He sounded weak too. "It's been terrible. My stomach was so upset that my balls were almost in my mouth." The balls-and-mouth expression was Happy's favourite.

I laughed. "You don't remember eating anything foul?"

"*Yaar*, maybe the chilli chicken I ate last weekend is the culprit. I knew something was wrong with it. I had started farting after only half an hour of eating it."

"Have you been taking medicines?"

"Yes, yes, for a long time. It's not the first time that this problem has occurred."

"So?"

He looked like he was hiding something embarrassing. This was new. Happy was never embarrassed about anything.

"What is it, Happy?" I asked, concerned. Before reaching his place, I had been itching to tell him about Tamanna. But now she must wait, I realised.

"I don't think this is happening only because of my eating habits," he said hesitantly.

"Is there something else? Some other problem?"

"Yeah man," he sounded sad. "Actually I think this is also a major reason for my stomach trouble." With that, he slightly lifted himself up in the bed and settled into a peculiar posture, with his pelvis thrust out. "See, when I masturbate," he continued, "I hold my dick like this," he wrapped his fingers around the TV remote to show me how, "and the muscles of my stomach get stretched." His expression was dead serious. "Then, when I come, I get pushed forward by the pressure, and already my posture is wrong. So overall, it's a lot of pressure on my stomach muscles."

I couldn't control myself any longer and burst out laughing. "From where the hell did you get this idea, asshole?" I asked when I finally caught my breath.

"Shut up, man, it's a serious situation."

"Whatever," I said. I pitied the doctor who was treating him. Had Happy told him about this extraordinary self-diagnosis? I hoped not. I'd come to Happy to discuss my situation with Tamanna with him, but instead, I had become a victim of his bizarre stomach problem. Without wasting any more time, I came to the topic, "Listen, man, I want to tell you something . . ."

I poured out my heart to him. Happy listened to me quietly. After I was done, he remained quiet for some time, brooding. Then he said, "Wow, *yaar*, I'd never thought you'd fall in love again. You have always loved your wife so much. But, you know, I have always believed that the human heart has an endless supply of love. One can fall in love with one more person for sure. And from what I have gathered, she seems to have something for you as well."

"Thanks, man. That means a lot to me."

"It's a tricky situation because you are both married. But if destiny has brought you together, then there must be something in it," he added. "And Tamanna seemed like a very nice person when I met her last year at your party. Otherwise I would have scolded you. I'm not the kind of friend who would let his buddy put his dick anywhere he wants to."

Yes, that's my friend Happy for you.

On my way back home later, I purposely chose to walk slowly. I wanted to be with Tamanna and her thoughts for some more time. Back home, a totally different world awaited me. When I reached there, I stopped before going inside and looked up at the sky. For some moments I kept standing there.

I'd read somewhere that sound can never be destroyed. I decided to test the truth of this claim.

"Tamanna, I love you," I murmured to the thin air around me. "Can you hear the voice of this stupid man?"

With that, I climbed the stairs to my house, where my wife and daughter waited for me.

6

April 10, 2009—the day my first book, *The Gross Injustice*, was launched—came after a long wait. The event happened at India International Centre, Delhi and was a big hit. The chief guest was an ex-cabinet minister who had been honoured with both the Padma Shri and the Padma Vibhushan. I had no way to reach such a prominent personality. It was Vikas who arranged it all.

Vikas had been my batchmate in school. We stayed in touch for a couple of years after passing out through occasional calls. But soon, the period between the calls expanded and eventually we lost touch. Then, one day in 2007, quite out of the blue, I received a call from him. We were talking after a long time. He told me he had been going through his old contact list and had randomly dialled my number to see how I was. I was really glad to hear his voice. We spoke about our school days and, at the end, decided to meet for dinner.

Over dinner, we gave each other our life's update and generally had a good time. The chemistry we shared in school was somehow still alive. We remained constantly in touch after that. In April 2009, when I spoke to him about the book launch, he was quite forthcoming in helping me find a celebrity for the event. He happened to know a civil servant who worked in the Parliament House. When

Vikas contacted him, he put us in touch with the minister, who, in turn, readily agreed to be a part of my big day. His presence brought in the media too, which helped in making the book launch a really grand affair. I am grateful to Vikas for his help till this day.

At the event, Sangini and I together welcomed everyone at the gate. One by one, the guests trickled in and congratulated us. But my eyes waited for someone special. There was only one question on my mind: *Tamanna, where are you?*

Finally, she came. And my heart leapt with joy. Today she was going to see me launch my book. It was going to be moment of great pride for me. Today was my chance to impress her.

With Sanjay by her side, Tamanna walked down the corridor, looking breathtaking in an elegant yellow-coloured chiffon sari that complimented the delicate contours of her body. It was the first time I was seeing her in a sari. I had a hard time deciding whether she looked more attractive in jeans and top—her usual attire—or in a sari. It was a close call, but the sari won. When she and Sanjay reached us, she congratulated me generously. Her eyes were shining bright with happiness. Then she gave Sangini—who was looking as stunning as her in a white cotton suit with a big dark-brown bindi and kohled eyes—a big hug. I beamed at seeing the two of them hug.

Just then, Sanjay patted my back and I had to turn to attend to him. I shook his hand and waited for him to congratulate me. But the pompous pig simply walked inside. He did not have the courtesy to even wish me. *Was he jealous?* I wondered.

Soon the chief guest arrived and we started the event. It was well received and we managed to sell all the copies of the book we had arranged for at the venue. The launch was followed by tea and snacks, during which the guests interacted with each other. Some newspaper reporters interviewed me, and my friends and family wished me luck. The whole time I exchanged pleasantries with everyone and thanked them for coming, I kept stealing glances at Tamanna.

Come talk to me, Tamanna, the words echoed inside my mind. *Touch my book, hold it in your hands, wish me luck.*

Tamanna came to me with Sanjay after half the guests had left. To my delight, she was carrying a copy of the book.

She congratulated me again and said, "This is only the first milestone, Arjun. The next one would be to make this book a huge best-seller."

"Yes, indeed!" I said.

Sanjay kept smiling all the while. He didn't say anything. But it didn't matter. Tamanna had spoken to me and said that the book may become a best-seller. What more could I want?

***

From the very next day, I started getting emails about the book from different parts of India. Some of the letters praised the book, some others enquired when I was writing my next book, while a few expressed disappointment and criticism. I was happy with the response, but when I contacted the publishers, I was told that the sales were low. They told me that thick books like *The Gross Injustice* were always hard to sell as they catered only to a small audience. Sangini had warned me about this but I had not heeded her advice. I was hesitant to cut down on the word count, wanting to keep the message and the experience of the book intact.

A few days later, Babbu came to me in the office. He was smiling wickedly. I understood he was in the mood for fun. Finally, he had gotten over the disappointment of not being able to find Simmi.

"You look lost, *mere yaar*. No word from Bhabhiji, huh?" he asked.

No, there had been none. I was eagerly waiting to hear Tamanna's feedback. Sangini and I were going to their place the following weekend. Maybe then she'd tell me what she thought of the book. I desperately hoped she had finished reading the book by then. But had she even begun reading it? What if she had tossed it aside on reaching home? What if she had forgotten . . .

Then I realised: "Bhabhiji"! *The bastard!*

"You do your work, okay?" I tried to dismiss Babbu.

"Oh come on, fucker! I can't see you like this," he replied. "Okay, let's do one thing. It's 10.30 right now. Come, I'll take you to her to ask her one thing."

A smiled crept up my face. "What'll you ask her, loser?"

Babbu looked serious *and* even more funny. "I'll ask her, Arjun, yes I'll definitely ask her. 'Listen, Tamanna Bhabhi, why haven't you given any feedback for his book? After all, that's your book too.'"

Tragedy King Dilip Kumar! I laughed despite myself.

The next second, my cell phone rang. It was an unknown number. I took the call. The first "hello" from the other side had me fumbling.

"Ye-ye-yes?" I replied.

Gosh! Was it her?

"Hi, Arjun, this is Tamanna."

Oh God! What should I do? OH GOD! Thanks! Thanks, thank you so much!

OH MY GOD!

"Hey, is it Tamanna?" Babbu whispered.

I nodded in return. This was the first time she was calling me. I couldn't find my speech.

"Hello? Are you there, Arjun?" she checked.

"Yek, I-I mean, yes, I am he-he-here," I fumbled again.

In front of me, Babbu had started dancing stupidly. I put my hand on the phone and ordered him to get out of the room. "Get out! Go out, you jerk."

"Wow, man, *ladki ka phone aaya to dost ko bhool gaya!*" he said and ran out.

I quickly put the phone back against my ear. "What's happening?" Tamanna was asking. "Everything okay? Arjun?"

"Yeah, yeah, everything o-okay . . . You tell me?" My heart was hammering inside my chest.

"I am good," she said. I could sense she was smiling. "I had to call you, Arjun. I took your number from Sangini. I finished reading your book last night. And from today onwards, I am your biggest fan. Till date I haven't read this kind of stuff."

I became numb with happiness. I couldn't get any words out. It felt like I had found my destiny. Now I could die in peace.

"You are truly a gifted writer, Arjun," Tamanna continued. "I was never aware you had this side too. Honestly, I want to salute you for writing such an incisive and brilliant book."

Ohmygodisthisreallyhappening?

"You are being too generous, Tamanna," I managed to squeak.

"I am not, Arjun. If you are the author of this book, which of course you are, then I'm grateful that you are my . . . umm . . . my husband's friend."

Oh no! "My friend," not "my husband's friend"! I must correct that. I took a deep breath. My hands were trembling. "Why only Sanjay's, Tamanna, am I not your friend too?"

Tamanna laughed. "Of course you are. I mean, okay, we are friends too."

Then there was an awkward pause as both of us struggled to think of what to say next. I really wanted to keep the conversation alive. I never wanted it to end. I frantically searched for a topic to introduce. Just then, Tamanna spoke up.

"Uhh, I am sorry, somebody's at the door. I'll have to disconnect."

No, no, no, no! Please stay on and talk to me!

"Oh all right," I said, disheartened. "Let's talk later . . ."

"Sure. I've many questions from the book, and I would be delighted if you could answer those for me. So, let's talk at length whenever we meet next. I got to rush now. Goodbye!" She disconnected even before I could say goodbye, and Lionel Richie returned to me.

> *Tell me how to win your heart,*
> *For I haven't got a clue.*

As soon as I put the phone in my pocket, Babbu re-entered the room. The jerk had been watching me from outside the entire time. He said, "Sir, may I present to you Happiness Unplugged again?" With that, he resumed his stupid dancing.

I shook my head and sat down to watch Babbu's self-choreographed act. With every second, his steps became more and more absurd. By the end, I couldn't tell whether he was dancing or simply jumping around because his groin had been injured. He stopped only when I started laughing uncontrollably.

"Hey, I am doing this after fifteen years!" he said. "And I'm sure even now I am not as funny as you were back then."

He was right. Fifteen years ago, I used to drink like army men, eat like Punjabis, and dance like Sunny Deol. During parties, I would be the funniest dancer on the floor. In my long pointed shoes, tight black jeans, and fitted yellow T-shirt, I looked like a drunk cockatoo too wounded to fly. In those days, I used to worship Michael Jackson and wanted to become like him. But all I could manage to become was the butt of all jokes.

When Babbu finally sat down, I told him all that Tamanna had said on phone.

"Well going, man! Next you know she, like Simmi, would be asking you to fuck her."

I threw a pen at him. It hit him on his shoulder. "Ouch!" he exclaimed and returned to his desk.

I know Babbu meant it only as a joke, but the idea was dirty and derogatory. I could never think about Tamanna that way. If the joke had come from a stranger, I would have picked up a fight. But, since it had come from my best friend, what choice did I have but to forgive and forget?

Just then I received a message from my other best friend, Happy. *Is it my fault that you have started having sex with your maid in sheer desperation????*

Sending nonsenscial messages like these at the oddest hours was Happy's habit.

"Internet speed is a bit slow," Babbu complained after some time. "Are you downloading something?"

"Hmmm, yeah," I replied.

"What?"

I shook my head and smiled.

"What happened? Why are you smiling?" Babbu asked. "Wait, are you watching some porno site?"

"Shut the fuck up!"

Babbu swiftly got up and walked to my desk.

"Michael Jackson?" he asked in surprise.

I had been downloading the video of Michael Jackson's "The Way You Make Me Feel." When I was in school, that song used to run in my veins.

"How many years has it been since you last heard him?" Babbu asked.

"When I was seventeen?" I guessed.

"It's fucking true. Love makes you a bloody horny teenager again," Babbu said and returned to his seat.

71

7

A few days later, I exited the office after a hectic day, humming an old Michael Jackson number. On my way to the parking lot, I constantly stared at Deepika Padukone's poster on the side of Satyam Cineplex.

This had become my routine. Every day, while going to and returning from office, I would feast on that poster, satisfying my thirsty eyes. It was my only way of seeing Tamanna regularly. As yet, I had not been able to procure a photograph of her. Daily, I thanked the cosmetic company for putting that poster up there. As a token of gratitude, I had been buying that company's products for Sangini and myself for weeks now. I had even been recommending their cosmetic line to my friends. That day, before getting into the car, I stopped and stared some more at the poster as if I was a lost desert traveller and that poster was an oasis on the horizon. In the depths of Deepika's face, I saw Tamanna's features. Ever since the day she'd called me in office, I had not had any contact with her.

From the poster, I looked down at my right hand, which had forever secured Tamanna's sweat in it. I brought it to my lips and kissed it.

Oh God! Oh Almighty! Help me please!

My eyes became moist. I was caught in a hopeless situation. On one hand, there was Tamanna, whom I could never have, and on the other, was Sangini, whom I still loved with all my heart. I wished that Tamanna was there to wipe away my tears . . .

"Hi Arjun Uncle," a familiar voice called me from behind.

I turned around to find her standing there with her son.

GOD HAS LISTENED TO ME!

"Hi, Vicky . . ." I murmured.

Tamanna was staring at my face. I realised my eyes were still moist. I tried to blink away my tears. My pulse quickened. I was already sweating. Tamanna glanced at the poster on my left and returned her gaze to me. "What were you doing, Arjun?" she asked, confused.

Oh crap! Has she been here all this while?

I had to quickly recover from the sudden shock and think of a clever response. To buy time, I closed my car's door and walked up to them. "Hey, nothing! There's my office at the back and here's this beautiful poster that I was watching while passing. That's all. What a pleasant surprise by the way!" This was the best I could manage.

"So, you are a fan of Deepika Padukone, is it?"

I bobbed my head up and down in response. *No, I am your fan, Tamanna!*—my mind echoed.

"Something wrong with your eyes? They are red . . ."

Fuck! "Oh really?" I started rubbing my eyes. "They have been itching since morning. I'll put some eye drops at home." Then, desperate to change the topic, I questioned, "What are you doing here?"

"I wanted to shop. And Vicky wanted to eat at McDonald's," she explained. But she still looked confused. She seemed to be struggling to understand what I had been really doing a few moments ago. I felt like a small child who'd been caught red-handed by his teacher.

Suddenly, it dawned upon me. Tamanna was more beautiful than Deepika. It was right in front of my eyes. Tamanna's beautiful eyes, her glowing dusky complexion, her well-shaped pink lips, her sharp nose—it was all much more attractive than that photoshopped picture of Deepika.

"Phone," Tamanna's words brought me back to reality.

"Sorry?" I asked.

"Your phone, Arjun, it's ringing. What's up with you?"

"Oh!" Embarrassed, I took out my ringing phone. It was Sangini. Last night we had had an argument over a petty issue. I needed a quiet corner to write, but Sangini wanted to watch *How I Met Your Mother* on TV. That was the only series she followed and the only bit of TV she watched in the whole day. Otherwise, her day passed in household chores and in looking after our daughter. I should have understood this and waited for the episode to get over. Instead, I had shouted at her for not respecting my writing and not giving me enough space. I had told her that my writing was important for the whole family as the sales of my books could really help us financially. After that, we'd moved to some other old issues and finally it had become a big fight. Afterwards, on realising my mistake, I had apologised to her. And even though Sangini had forgiven me, she had remained upset. Even in the morning, she had seemed cold and had hardly spoken a word to me.

I picked up the phone, expecting to hear an upset Sangini. But, to my surprise, she sounded normal. She said she wanted to have something from outside for dinner. It was relieving to know she was in a better mood. I told her I'd get something nice.

"How's Sangini?" Tamanna asked as I disconnected the call.

"Oh she's well. Wants to eat something from outside."

"So what are you going to take for her?"

Suddenly an idea struck me. Tamanna had said Vicky wanted to eat at McDonald's and Sangini was fond of their burgers. "I think I'll pick something from McDonald's only."

"Oh great. We were on our way there. Why don't you join us?"

My plan had worked! "Sure," I said. I quickly locked my car and we started walking together.

On our way, I told Tamanna about my argument with Sangini. She was glad to know that everything had ended well.

McDonald's was crowded as usual. Tamanna asked Vicky to occupy a table and the two of us walked to the counter. Tamanna was reluctant to let me pay for her, but when I insisted, she relented. The staff promptly began collecting and packing our junk food. I silently cursed them for being so quick about it. The faster they completed our order, the sooner I would have to leave. I had limited time!

By now, my heartbeat had normalised, but my body was still tense. I was standing so close to Tamanna and there was neither Sanjay nor Sangini to watch us. Just then, a man nudged us to get close to the counter and my hand brushed against Tamanna's and a shock of electricity ran through my body. I got goosebumps. But Tamanna seemed relaxed, in fact she seemed more at ease than usual.

"Arjun," she spoke up. "I'm impressed by how you handled the situation with Sangini yesterday."

"Thanks," I replied, smiling.

She continued, "We all have our share of good days and bad days. And we're all selfish. For instance, you didn't see why Sangini had to watch TV exactly at the time you wanted to write, and Sangini couldn't understand why you couldn't write after her episode got over. But that's completely okay as long as you learn from your actions. You both are as mortal, as weak, as strong, as wise, as ridiculous, and as human as everybody else on earth. We all have our own realities, our own priorities. Sometimes our wishes and our thoughts take precedence over everything else. That's how we're all made. None of us is perfect. Oh God, I've gotten all philosophical, I am sorry. I get carried away sometimes. Hey look, our order's done!"

Damn! So fast!

I smiled and picked the tray up and together we walked to the table Vicky had occupied. Tamanna's words had greatly impressed me. Not only was she intelligent and stunning, she was compassionate too. She had said that none of us is perfect. But, to me, she seemed absolutely perfect.

After placing Tamanna's and Vicky's burgers on the table, I picked my packet up and started to leave. In that moment, I was torn between two desires. I wanted to spend more time with Tamanna and, at the same time, I wanted to rush back to my wife and have dinner with her.

I must have looked lost for Tamanna said, "Is something wrong, Arjun?"

"Err . . . No, nothing!" Suddenly, an idea struck me. Kaleva Sweets, near Connaught Place, had introduced special fruit ice creams recently. They were actually full fruits, like apples or mangoes, with extremely delicious ice-cream in the centre. I don't know how they managed to make the fruits look uncut and whole after adding the ice cream, but the dessert tasted great and Sangini loved it. "Actually, I was thinking of taking ice cream for Sangini from Kaleva, CP." *Do you like ice creams too, Tamanna?*

"Oh, great. You must rush then. You have a long ride ahead of you."

She was right. Kaleva was twelve miles from my place, in

the opposite direction, and it was the peak rush hour. I was tired too after a long day at work. But none of it mattered. Distance? Time? Exhaustion? They had no meaning where Sangini's happiness was concerned.

"Yeah, bye! See you. We got to talk about my book."

"Yes, yes," she said. "Some other time. Thanks for the burgers! Bye!"

Fortunately, the drive was not as long as I'd anticipated. I found most of the signals green and the roads relatively uncrowded. Instead of sixty minutes, I took only twenty-five minutes to reach Kaleva. *Today is my lucky day!*

Sangini was delighted to see the surprise dessert. She gulped down every bit of it like a small child. Watching her eat like that made me immensely happy.

"Hey, want some more?" I asked when she finished.

"Not today," she answered. "I am sooooo full." She laughed. I laughed with her.

After that, she went to bed and I started my writing. I wrote for an hour and then went to the bedroom to find my wife and daughter—my two princesses, my universe—peacefully sleeping together. Very quietly, I closed the door and tiptoed to the bed. I planted a kiss on both their heads and went to sleep.

I dozed off thinking about Sangini, and had a beautiful dream about Tamanna. When I woke up the next day, it was to find Sangini curled up against me. I started running my fingers through her hair. In my mind was the dream I had seen of Tamanna. With my wife lying beside me, I was missing another woman. I should have felt some pangs of guilt, but there were none . . .

8

I was trying to search for a record, the one with my dad's favourite song in it. I neither remembered the band nor the name of the song, but I was sure I would recognise it if I saw it. Tamanna was with me, looking stunning as always. I desperately wanted her to listen to the track. We searched long and hard, but without success. Finally, Tamanna said, "Arjun, you yourself know the song. Why don't you sing it for me?"

"I don't remember the song," I said, sadly.

She smiled and walked closer to me. She held my hand and said, "I know you have a bad memory, but what I also know is that today you will gift me this song. Come on, sing it."

The next moment I started singing it. Suddenly, I knew not only the song's name and tune, but also the lyrics, right till the last line. When I finished, Tamanna laughed and clapped and came closer to me and . . . I woke up. It was 5.45 a.m.

In 1970s, when my dad was still alive, our home used to constantly reverberate with English and Hindi songs playing on our HMV record player. Although I had very little understanding of English songs at such a tender age, I started developing a fair taste for them.

I lost my father to brain tumour at the age of seven.

At that time, my mom worked on a high post in a government department. After dad, she became the rock on which I grew up. She worked hard day and night to educate me well and keep me comfortable. Her hair became white more than a decade before they generally do in women.

My dad also served in a government department on a very high post. With him, life was full of outings, movies, and holidays. But after he died, everything stopped. We spent only on the most necessary things.

When I was a child, I never really missed my father much. That was because I had my cousins and friends.

By the time I reached my 20s, however, I started feeling a vacuum inside my heart. That vacuum was filled when Sanghmitra was born and I myself became a father.

Anyway, after my dad's demise, our record player too stopped working. My mom took it to the repair shop once, but it couldn't be made functional again. It was as if it had died with my father and couldn't be brought back to life. As a result, the wooden shelf that so proudly housed the countless records that my father had collected over the decades, started gathering dust from disuse. Our house became quiet. Instead of music, now a solemn silence of mourning hung over it constantly. Slowly, the memory of the lovely songs I used to hear all day started fading away from my mind. Over time, I forgot almost all the records, barring perhaps a couple of albums of Boney M. and Abba.

I sat upright on my bed. The song's tune and lyrics were still echoing in my head. It had been nearly thirty years since I last heard it. I had been seven and didn't even understand the lyrics at the time. I'd thought I had no memory left of the track. Maybe I'd have recognised it if I had heard it play anywhere, but even then I'd have heard it as one hears a new song. Then how had I been able to sing it in my dreams?

Am I still dreaming? Is this real?

I turned my head towards my wife and daughter. They were still fast asleep. So, slowly and quietly, I got up from the bed and walked out of the room. I tiptoed to my study room and booted my computer. I logged in to YouTube and typed, "so happy together by the turtles."

The name was correct! I clicked on the link with the most views and the video started buffering. I put on my headphones and when the song began, I lip-synced with it till the end. I didn't miss a single word. It was almost a miracle. Even after the song ended, I kept sitting in my chair, staring at the computer screen in awe. It was unreal.

What was Tamanna doing to me?

I kept humming the tune for the whole day. It was indeed a beautiful song, filled with love. I understood why it was my dad's favourite.

> *Imagine me and you, I do,*
> *I think about you day and night,*
> *It's only right,*
> *To think about the girl you love,*
> *And hold her tight,*
> *So happy together.*
> *I can't see me loving nobody but you,*
> *For all my life.*

At office the next day, I kept thinking about the dream and the song. My love for Tamanna was bringing back memories I had long forgotten. It was a magical experience. I wished I could call and tell her about how much she was influencing me. But, alas, I could not. Apart from our formal family meetings, all that we had shared so far was one phone call and two stray meetings—that's it.

I took out my cell phone from my shirt pocket and opened the received calls log. It still had Tamanna's number, a beautiful thing. I softly moved my fingers over the number on the screen, remembering our conversation. Goosebumps erupted on my arms and neck.

From that day onwards, it became even more difficult for me to remain without her, to be unable to talk to her and hear her beautiful voice whenever I wanted (and that was always), to accept the fact that there was zero possibility of our getting together, that there was no way I could see her beautiful face every day . . . True I saw Deepika's poster, but that was too little to satiate me—only a morsel of bread for a starving man.

Then an idea struck me.

There was a Baskin Robbins near my office. I had never visited it, for I dislike the brand. In my opinion, their ice creams are too expensive and servings too small. But now was the time to change my opinion. It had struck me that from the glass window that covered the eastern wall of the outlet, one should be able to see the Deepika poster clearly. I got up like a man on a mission and rushed to the shop. My guess was right. The poster was right out there, big and pretty. I ordered a chocolate-chip scoop and sat chose a table from where I had a good view of the poster. I took my time finishing the ice cream as the poster soothed my famished heart.

This became my routine. Every day after lunch, I would steal away from the office on the pretext of buying something or making a private phone call or to just breathe fresh air. I hid this from Babbu. He was a great pal, but I wanted to see Tamanna in the absence of any known eyes, with ease and without disturbance.

During these daily visits, I had some moments of guilt, when I would think, *"Oh God! I am married. I have a family. But Tamanna remains with me all the time. She is married too. But I love her intensely and hopelessly. Please, God, help me. I love my wife,"* but they were few and far between and had no lasting impact.

***

A month after the dream, in mid-2009, Sanjay invited Sangini and me for dinner at their place. As always, we accepted the invitation readily and gladly, but I found myself wishing that *we* were hosting the dinner and not the Sahnis. This was because of two reasons. First, if they were hosting, Tamanna spent more time cooking in the kitchen and attending to other household chores. Even though I liked seeing her in her housewife avatar, it meant that I got to interact less with her. Second, Sanjay tended to boast more when he was at his place. With Tamanna constantly moving about, he found it easier to burden Sangini and me with stories of his past achievements, stories that we had by now memorised through and through.

I had drawn a couple of inferences from Sanjay's stories. To begin with, I had become certain that he exaggerated a lot and magnified his accomplishments. I respected him for being a successful man but hated him for being a braggart. Sometimes, I even doubted if he had really achieved all that he boasted of because, according to me, if a person has overcome a lot of hurdles in his life, he should be modest and humble, and not a boastful arrogant oaf. I pitied Tamanna for having a husband like him. The few hours I spent with Sanjay in a week were enough to test my patience. To think that Tamanna had to spend every night and morning with him made me want to pull her into a big hug and never let her go.

Many of Sanjay's stories described how he was betrayed by people whom he had considered his best friends. He narrated how most of his friends had eaten and drank with him for months and years and then had abandoned him when he was in trouble. I did not blame his friends for maintaining a relationship of convenience with him. The way Sanjay behaved, he *asked* to be betrayed and hurt. Even I would have broken up my friendship with him had I not fallen in love with his extraordinary wife.

So basically, Sanjay's company was a pain in the neck. When he talked, he was a torture; and when Tamanna, Sangini, and I would be talking about something logical and relevant, he would interrupt and divert the conversation towards himself. When he told his stories, they would be filled with lies and unbelievable facts, and when I told my stories, he would respond condescendingly. Often I would abuse him in my mind.

Sanjay, you liar, you duffer, you asshole, you don't deserve my beautiful and smart Tamanna. You are a useless and boastful dog, but your wife is fantastic and fabulous and I love her.

The same thing happened that evening. We were all drinking Bloody Mary and eating cookies when I started talking about how I used to help my mother in the kitchen when I was young. I was an only child and my mom had to take care of everything after my father's demise. So out of my love and concern for her, I would help her a lot.

"I helped her in cooking, buying groceries, cutting vegetables, washing the dishes, cleaning the house, folding clothes, everything," I was saying.

To this Sanjay responded, "When I was a child, my servants took care of these things." Then he laughed.

Bastard!

I looked at Sangini and found her expressionless. Tamanna,

on the other hand, smiled and said, "I wish Vicky helps me as much when he grows up!"

Later, during dinner, Sanjay narrated an old story of how he had excelled and gotten promoted at one of his jobs at a world-famous MNC. He concluded the story with, "Now see, here I am, making more money than my boss used to make at the time."

At the time, he was managing a primary school his parents had started. But I never heard him talking about his current work. I had never seen him attending work-related calls either. I had passed the school a couple of times in my car and each time I had found him standing outside and smoking. It did not look like he worked really hard to keep the school running. That was his parents' job.

"That's very impressive, Sanjay," I said, because I had to say something. "Soon you will have a Mercedes parked in your garage."

"Yeah, man!" he replied. "I hope you at least get a Maruti Esteem for wishing for my Mercedes." He laughed again.

Son of a bitch!

"I don't understand why people buy big cars," Sangini chimed in. "To be honest, we are very happy with our cosy Santro."

Whoa, this was new!

I looked at Tamanna and found her chewing her food angrily, her eyes fixed on her husband. But, unfortunately, he wasn't looking at her.

Later, on our way back home, Sangini exploded, "What does he think of himself? Next time I see him, I will shoot him. He is a dog. He tries to make you feel small. Bloody idiot has no idea how much better a man you are. He is lucky to be your friend!"

I was speechless. I should have felt as infuriated with Sanjay as Sangini was, but I was delighted! Sangini had not only taken a stand on my behalf in front of Sanjay, she was also mad at him for trying to belittle me because of my financial failures. This was a big change. Ever since I had disclosed my career failures to her, she had never supported me like this. She was always full of criticism and barbs for me.

I looked at her lovingly. Somehow, she looked prettier when she was cross with someone. Suddenly, Michael Bolton came to my head.

Tell me how am I supposed to live without you?
Now that I have been lovin' you so long.

"His wife is so much better than him. She is so sweet and gentle and respectful and caring and smart. I don't know why she married him. The only reason I go to their place is her."

Same here! I wish I could say that. But I had to answer smartly. If Sangini got too pissed with Sanjay, the get-togethers might end completely. And that was one thing I was scared of the most.

"Hey, it's okay. Sanjay is like that. He does not realise he is being rude. And I don't mind his comments so much. There is a lot to learn from him as well. And Tamanna, as you said, is great."

That night, after a long time, I kissed my wife goodnight and shared some intimate moments with her.

Then I turned and said in my mind, "Goodnight to you too, Tamanna. Missing you."

9

One day in June 2009, I had a night of troubled sleep. I had dreams about my childhood, my school, and my friends. While I couldn't exactly remember most of them, when I woke up I felt heavy and low. It was as if someone had kept a huge burden on my heart while I was asleep.

I thought the feeling would disappear soon. But it did not. I called up Babbu to ask if he wanted to drive to the office with me. He said he would get late and asked me to go ahead on my own. He would come later.

I was so weirded out that day that I didn't even look at Deepika's poster on my way to office. When I sat down at my desk, I didn't feel like working. I wondered if it had something to do with Tamanna. To help myself, I again tried to recall what I had seen in my dreams. Just then Happy called. Usually, his calls cheered me up. But that day, I was irritated and in no mood to talk.

What is he calling about at ten in the morning? The bastard doesn't work and doesn't let others work either!

"Arjun, did you read it?" Happy sounded sad. Something was wrong. This wasn't the usual Happy. For a mad moment, I wondered if someone had stolen his phone and was calling me. But, no, I could recognise his voice.

"Heard what, Happy?" I asked. "Everything okay?"

"Michael died, man! He . . . It's over!" I heard him break down at the other end.

I was shocked. Michael Dull Force was a common friend of ours. He had met Happy in the mid-1990s, when Happy used to play Junior County in England. In 2004, Michael had come to India and had even stayed at my place for a couple of days.

"What? I chatted with him only last week! How?"

"Wh-what? I'm talking about Michael Jackson!"

A cold shiver travelled down my spine. I was speechless. Like a robot, I disconnected Happy's call and googled the news. It was all over the Internet. It was true.

Two decades ago, when I was a teenager, Michael Jackson was my idol. For hours together, I used to practise his dance steps. I would watch his videos and try to imitate his style and body language. I would have no qualms about who might be watching me. When I would walk down the neighbourhood, I would moonwalk. I had life-size posters of the King of Pop on my room's walls.

The first time I watched Michael Jackson was on August 25, 1984, in the video of "Thriller." A friend of mine owned its big black cassette. Those were the glorious days of Amitabh Bachchan, Rajesh Khanna, Jeetendra, and Dharmendra. But we had witnessed nothing as amazing as MJ. In the coming years, I became obsessed with Jackson and his moves.

In 1988, I borrowed eight rupees from my childhood friend Bobby to buy Jackson's latest *Bad*. I had ten rupees with myself and the cassette cost eighteen rupees. When we both had the money, we ran to the store. There were about forty odd guys like us already there. It took us five minutes to make the purchase. We rushed back to my home and quickly placed the cassette inside my Sony deck. Within fifteen minutes, I'd gone crazy. "The Way You Make Me Feel" played on loop the whole day in my home.

Now, this hero of my childhood, this god of millions around the world, was dead. I felt like someone had snatched away a part of my past, my youth, from me, leaving me incomplete. *Was this the reason I had been feeling low since the morning?* Tears welled up in my eyes.

"What happened, sir, why are you crying?"

I never noticed when Prakash, our office boy, had entered the cabin with my morning tea. He looked concerned.

"Oh nothing." It was awkward. "You won't understand . . . I am okay. Thanks."

In normal circumstances, I would have asked Prakash to not mention the incident to anyone, but at the time, it didn't matter to me.

I sat there feeling numb for some time, unable to think anything clearly. Then, suddenly and mysteriously, it all came back to me—the visions I had seen in my dreams at night. I had dreamt about my childhood friends, the games I used to play with them, the fights we were always having, the scolding we got every day. How we all ran around the neighbourhood and danced to Michael Jackson tracks and noticed the pretty girls of our locality and rode around on our father's scooters. We were a group of four and were both famous and infamous on our street.

These were all pleasant visions for sure, but then why was I feeling low? Was it only nostalgia? The answer was no.

Three years ago, in 2006, I had cut off my friends from my life. It was a result of the realisation that I couldn't depend on them in times of need. I should have realised that a long time ago, but I was too simple-minded to see through my friends' behaviour.

Like all friends, we used to have fights often. But then we would patch up too within no time. But as we grew up, the patching-up stopped happening unless I made efforts. I also start feeling that the three took advantage of me. They often laughed at me and made me a *bakra*. I was contacted if they had any work, but if I had some work they would pretend to be busy. I was the one who held the group together, but I was treated awfully by all of them.

Sangini had often warned me about their nature, but I had ignored her doubts and suspicions, thinking that my friends meant well and were genuinely busy in their lives. Then, one night in 2006, I had severe pain in my chest. Sangini rushed me to the hospital, where the doctors admitted me immediately. I SMSed my friends about the incident, hoping they would be there to support and help Sangini and my mother. Happy and Babbu came at once, but my other three friends never appeared. One of them was not in Delhi and the other two were too busy with "stuff." Thankfully, the chest pain was a result of severe indigestion. But that day I understood the truth of the proverb, "A friend in need is a friend indeed." After I recovered, I sent a text to all three of them to inform them that they no longer existed in my lives. In response, they made some half-hearted calls and messaged a couple of times, but for the first time in my life I didn't send a reply. Since then, I had had no contact with them.

Sitting in my office that day, I realised that I missed them. There was a vacuum inside my heart where they had made their place. Sure they hadn't been the best of friends, but we had our good moments too. Maybe I had been at fault too, maybe I had misunderstood them, maybe they really were busy in their lives. Michael Jackson's untimely death made me realise that life is too short for holding grudges and losing friends. Then

I thought, if Tamanna can love Sanjay, I could definitely make peace with my friends.

My eyes remained moist throughout the day. The heaviness I had been feeling because of my dream had lifted, but it had been replaced by a bigger weight that seemed to be pulling me down. I had never thought that the death of my childhood idol thousands of miles away would affect me so much. As the day passed, my thoughts kept returning to my childhood. They were such carefree days, full of *masti* and laughter. We would sing and dance and party and eat all day.

It suddenly struck me that those days would never come back again, no matter how much the child in me yearned for them. This wasn't a new realisation—I had known it all along. But when I *consciously* thought about it, tears welled up in my eyes. I had become tired of everyday struggles and battles. I could have given up anything to just go back to that magical time and stay there forever. But alas. Time cannot be turned back. Now, I had to work hard so that Sanghmitra could have a memorable childhood.

At 4.45 p.m., my cell phone rang.

I hadn't saved the number, but I immediately recognised it. It was Tamanna. Seeing her number made me both happier and sadder.

"Hello," I said. Strangely, I was feeling completely normal. My heart was not beating wildly, my nerves were calm, things were not tumbling inside my stomach, my breathing was not laboured.

"Hi, it's me, Tamanna."

"I recognised your number."

"You sound very down. What happened?"

She had again sensed I was upset! "No . . . nothing," I tried to avoid it.

"Are you crying, Arjun? Or, um, were you . . . were you crying a while back?"

This time, I didn't respond, *could* not respond.

"Are you all right, Arjun?"

I want you to come running to me and hold me while I sob.

"Yeah . . ." I croaked.

"For God's sake, Arjun, what happened? I know you are not okay!"

I could not hold it in any longer. I poured out my heart. I told her everything—from how terrible I was feeling about MJ's death to how badly I was missing my teenage years and how tired I was of everyday battles. The vacuum inside my heart, the pain, the lost times—I told her most of it. She heard everything patiently and, in a soothing, gentle voice, said, "Wow, Arjun, this is rare."

A pause followed. I was already regretting letting my guard down. I shouldn't have lost control over myself like that.

She sensed that and said, "Thank you for sharing all this with me. It means you consider me your friend and I'm glad for that. I—" She paused again. *Is she checking her words? Go on, Tamanna, say it!* But, alas, she changed her route. "You know, Arjun, we all have our idols during our teenage years, but the kind of attachment you have with yours is rare. I mean, even Sanjay was a big fan of MJ. We all were, probably. He saw the news in the morning and went to office after that. I spoke to him twice on the phone later, but he showed no trace of any sadness. And that's how majority of people are. But you are not like everybody . . .

"We all forget whatever we do and hold dear in our teens. Responsibilities and realities take over our lives. After a certain age we all stop living; we just exist, within the confines of our work, family, daily routine. We lose our old friends, our heroes, our passions. But somewhere in our hearts, we keep craving to be the same again. Unfortunately, we are unable to do so because we have so many things to take care of. So most of us live superficial lives, wearing masks of sorts. But you seem to be . . . different."

I was at a loss of words. I didn't know what to do or say anymore.

Tamanna made it easier. "Arjun, if I ask you to do something, will you do it?"

I will jump out of that window if you ask me to. "Of course! Don't embarrass me."

"Promise?"

"Promise."

"Today, go to all your childhood friends and meet them. I am sure they too must be heartbroken after hearing this unfortunate news. Forget about all that has happened. Just go and give them a tight hug. And then sit down together and listen to your favourite MJ tracks."

My God, she is a much better person than I had thought.

"Okay, I will do that," I said.

"That's good. Let me know how it goes, okay?"

"Sure."

"Great. Now I must go." *NO!* "I have to buy—"

Stop her from going! Say something! Ask her why she called.

"Why did you call up?" I blurted out. *Wow!* "I mean to say, did you call me just like that or did you want to . . .?"

"Oh, I wanted to talk about your novel. Nothing important. Just that I was thinking about it, and I realised that it may not become a bestseller. Wait, don't get me wrong. It's a great book, but it says the truth in a brutal manner, and many people won't like that. Truth seldom sells, you know. You are a gifted writer, and I pray you sell millions of copies one day. But for that you must write for the masses. Once you have established yourself as a successful writer, you can write as many brilliant and thought-provoking books like *The Gross Injustice* as you like. But this is a delicate and crucial time in your writing career, and you must . . . Oh God, look at me, I must sound like an old woman; so preachy!"

"No, no! I get what you are trying to say, and I completely agree."

"Oh, you are sweet. But I must go now. It was nice talking to you."

"Likewise," I said.

"Bye."

"Goodbye."

She hung up. But I sat there holding the phone against my ear for a long time. This was her second call to me. It had to mean something, my heart said. Maybe after two years, she had finally started feeling something—the connection, the vibes.

Suddenly, I was immensely proud of my love for her. All the guilt was gone from me. If I had had any doubts remaining about my feelings being a mere crush, they were removed that day.

Whenever I thought about her after that day, I could feel an absolute serenity and calmness inside my heart. Being with her thoughts was like involuntarily visualizing the calm still waters of the ocean, standing in absolute silence, listening to the occasional sound of some sea bird, with waves washing my feet, and wind tangled in my hair.

10

I left office that day like a man with a purpose. In the morning, I had been feeling so low that I had not even glanced at Deepika's poster. Therefore, to make up for it, I went to Baskin Robbins in the evening and bought a double scoop of chocolate chip ice cream. As I sat down to eat it, my eyes never left the poster. In my mind, I kept replaying the conversation I'd had with Tamanna a couple of hours ago.

You are not like everybody. You seem to be different.

If I ask you to do something, will you do it?

On my way back home, I recalled all the fun times I had shared with my childhood friends. The oldest and the shortest amongst us was Harsh. Now employed as the marketing head at a leading mobile phone company, he used to be our sex guru during school days. He used to buy cheap erotic Hindi literature from a downtown shop and had the largest collection of *Debonair* magazine in the locality. While the other boys would feel embarrassed to ask the vendor for the magazine, Harsh was a close friend of the guy.

Bobby was the richest person in the group. His father worked at some senior position in the union government. He wore clothes that his relatives brought from the USA and the UK and was the only one with a free landline connection in the area. He would seldom permit us to use it, although he would screw it for hours talking to his girlfriend. He now worked as a senior manager at a leading bank

The stingiest of the four of us was Sameer, now the vice-president at a top brokerage firm. He would calculate the price of every slice of pizza he had and never paid one penny more than his share.

After parking my car near my house, I started walking towards Harsh's home instead of going inside. This used to be my routine during school days. Instead of going directly to my place after school, I would go to Harsh's or Bobby's or Sameer's place first to see if they were free and ready to play football or cricket. This routine continued for some months after we passed out from school. But after that our routines changed and we would hardly get time to meet during weekdays. So our get-togethers became weekend affairs, and if we had to meet, we would first call each other and plan it over the phone.

I walked up till Harsh's door and took a deep breath. I brought my finger to the doorbell . . . but then I had an idea. I walked back some steps, looked up at his balcony, and shouted out his name. I didn't need to call out twice. Harsh came out on the balcony within a couple of seconds, as if he was waiting for me to come. A minute later, the front door opened and we hugged. We didn't ask each other any of the million questions that came to our mind. I just said, "Let's go to Bobby's place?" He nodded.

The same thing happened at Bobby's place: He responded in a single call. From there, all three of us went to Sameer's compound. That bastard took three calls, but when he came out, his eyes were moist.

We got together at my place. Happy came too, with two wine bottles. We shared our memories and listened to MJ's songs. We talked about our obsessions and spoke about MJ's death. We were all emotional and happy at the same time. Everything was hilarious and everything was sad. Not for a moment it felt like we had not spoken to each other for three years. There was no awkwardness, no weird silences, only stupidity and laughter. After years, I had a rocking time with my friends.

And all this was because of Tamanna.

***

Next morning was a completely different world for me. I woke up with a huge smile on my face. While doing my morning chores, my mind was giving a running commentary to Tamanna about last night's events. Instead of using a bucket and mug to bathe like I used to do daily, I took a shower that day and even tried moon-walking. When dressing up, I played "The Way You Make Me Feel" on the music system.

Sangini was amused. She had been very surprised the previous night too, when I had suddenly rang the doorbell with my three friends behind me. After the party, she had said it was good I had reconnected with my friends. But she was curious to know how it had all happened. At that time, I should have told her about Tamanna's call, but somehow I didn't. I knew it was wrong of me to not tell her, I knew that eventually she'd get to know, but somehow I kept it a secret. In response, I had simply looked at her and smiled mysteriously, leaving her to interpret it the way she wanted.

On my way to work, I had this almost uncontrollable desire to call up Tamanna and tell her about the re-union with my friends. I wanted to speak out aloud the commentary I had been silently giving since morning. But then hundreds of questions invaded my mind.

Is it a valid enough reason to call her? What if she thinks I am piling on her? What if she thinks I am trying to flirt with her? What if she thinks I am taking advantage of the two simple phone calls she made to talk about my book? What if she gets pissed off and never calls me back?

No, I couldn't take that risk. Calling her up and showing my enthusiasm was likely to create doubts in her mind, and if that happened, my relationship with her might not move forward at all. She had taken two years to call me, and I didn't want to spoil that by behaving irresponsibly.

On reaching office, I found Babbu already there. Overflowing with excitement, I told him all about the previous day as soon as I sat down. After listening to me, he got up and went out without a word. I was confused. *What had just happened?*

Twenty minutes later, he returned with cold coffee, noodles, and pastries from the Nescafe outlet in the office complex. For everybody in the office. My best friend was treating everyone because of Tamanna's call!

Naturally, our staff members were surprised. When they enquired about the reason for the party, Babbu said, "Arjun had his seventh child from his third wife."

"So, what do you plan to do next?" He asked me as we sipped our cold coffees together in our cabin. "You two are moving in the right direction."

"What plans?" I asked.

"Man, plans of meeting, meeting outside. I mean, you want to take your story further, no?"

"No! I don't have anything to take further, man. Remember, she and I both have a family? I mean, I love Sangini, you know. And I love Sanghmitra more than I love her. Nothing can ever happen between me and Tamanna, I know that very well. I am just going to enjoy these feelings. Hopefully, they will go away one day."

"Damn you, man! Do you realise your love is so intense that someone or the other, either Sangini or Tamanna or that bastard Sanjay, is likely to learn your little secret sooner or later? You can't keep such things hidden for long, asshole."

"I will face whatever is written in my destiny."

"Fuck you and your philosophical thoughts. When Sanjay finds out about your feelings, then your destiny won't help you."

"How would Sanjay find out? I am not going to do anything silly."

"Look who's talking! You stare at Deepika's poster all the time!"

I had no defence against that.

"The son of a bitch doesn't want to take it forward. Why the hell did I treat everyone?"

11

Eight days had passed since MJ's death and my last conversation with Tamanna. I woke up with an absolutely famished heart. I was missing MJ terribly, and Tamanna even more than that. I could still hear his voice whenever I desired. But no such luck with hers.

My heart craved for her while I struggled through the usual morning chores.

I must speak to you. I want to hear your beautiful voice.

Fortunately, luck was on my side that day, because at the breakfast table, Sangini said, "It's been quite a while since we met Tamanna and Sanjay."

Her words were music to my ears. Suddenly the cheese inside the sandwich I was eating became delicious.

I suppressed my excitement and replied casually, "Yeah, the great and noble Sanjay is pretty busy, it seems."

"Yeah, maybe it's good only that we've not met. It gets difficult to tolerate him sometimes."

My mouth was full of sandwich (the cheese had somewhat lost its taste again), so I pleaded silently: *No! Please no. Don't think about that pig Sanjay! He is a necessary evil in our friendship with Tamanna. Ignore him. Please, don't change your mood now.*

Sangini got up and disappeared inside the kitchen, saying, "I forgot to give you the vanilla cake I baked yesterday. You came home so late . . ." She returned with a big slice. It hardly looked like a cake slice though. First, it appeared as if it had been made of brown clay. And, second, it was hard. Very hard. Hard enough to make it unsuitable for a friendly cake fight.

But still, I was delighted. Why? Because it meant that Sangini had forgiven me and was ready to move ahead. In the initial years of our marriage, she used to experiment with cooking to offer me a variety of meals. She knew I loved sampling different cuisines and new dishes, so she'd challenge herself to make me happy. But, after her breakdown and my big disclosure in 2006, she stopped this experimentation. This was why I greeted the sight of the rock-solid cake with a big smile and excitedly took the first bite. I tried to crack and crush it between my strong jaws, but without much success.

"It's gotten a little hard. I over-baked it, I guess. Was making it for the first time . . ." Sangini explained apologetically.

"It's a great first attempt. I like it," I said, trying to chew it. I meant it too. Her sincere effort meant so much to me.

"Shut up. I know it's hopeless!" She looked at me in mock-anger.

I smiled. "No, it's not! Look, I am taking another piece." With that, I bit another piece but it slipped out of my hand and went rolling on the floor like a piece of stone. We both burst out laughing. Sangini fetched me water and sat down again.

"So do you want to invite the Sahnis for dinner tomorrow?" I returned to the topic. "Sanjay is not always so bad."

"He is. But then Tamanna makes up for all his idiotic crap. I think we can invite them."

You are the best life-partner on earth.

"But I don't want to call up Sanjay. It's your responsibility to call up Tamanna. If she declines, let me know."

"Yes, sir," my beautiful wife said and went back to the kitchen.

I love you.

Guilt pangs returned to me as I got up to leave for office. What would happen if Sangini learns my secret? What if Babbu was right? What if my feelings for Tamanna were to leak out one day? My family would be devastated, I knew. Sangini may not be able to bear it. On my way to work, I kept thinking about this. By the time I reached Janakpuri, I was all shaken.

I didn't look at Deepika's poster that morning. Instead, I looked at the shop windows on my right, humming a Lionel Richie song. In one of the stores, I saw a mannequin display draped in a one-piece black satin dress. It looked ravishing.

It had been a long time since Sangini had bought anything new for herself. I went into the shop and enquired about the price of the dress.

"Eight thousand rupees," the saleswoman replied.

At one point in time, the dress would have been affordable for me. But now, I couldn't buy it. Feeling guilty and ashamed, I left the shop and reached my office. On the way, I scolded myself for not being able to buy even a dress for my wife. I felt really, really sad and resolved to work harder and increase my earnings.

I opened my mailbox to find a sales-related mail from my publishers waiting to be read. The sales of my book had been slow, but I was hoping that it would pick up soon. I didn't expect it to sell millions of copies, but surely enough for it to become a big bestseller. Meanwhile, I had started experiencing a strong urge to write my next book. But what and how? I had one subject in mind, based loosely on my own teenage years. I had even prepared a rough draft. But I had been struggling to start writing the main text. Every time I'd sit down to write, I'd find that my heart was not with my pen.

Could Tamanna help me in choosing the right subject? She had certainly seemed knowledgeable enough about what the market wanted and what kind of books one should write at the beginning of one's career. I decided to speak to her about it the next day and started working.

In the evening, I received an SMS from my daughter.

Papa, please bring Ginger Bread Boy by Enid Blyton from WordsWorth showroom for me.

Sanghmitra, like me, was fond of reading. I immediately replied: *Yes, I will, my doll.*

The SMS had made me upbeat. Happily, I stopped at the bookstore on my way back and bought the Enid Blyton book. I should have been home in the next thirty minutes, but it took me forty instead, because, on a whim, I took a detour to pass by Tamanna's house. I knew I was going to meet her the next day, but still I couldn't stop myself once the idea originated in my mind. I was starving for a glimpse of her and twenty-four hours seemed like an awfully long period of time. As I approached the house, I slowed down and prayed that Tamanna be out on the balcony or on the street. But she was nowhere to be seen. I was crestfallen. I really, really wanted to see her. Even if I could have seen her shadow, I would have been somewhat satisfied.

Just then, a thought flashed like lightening through my mind. *What if Sanjay sees you here? Such a cheap act you are doing! A roadside romeo roaming around the house of a married woman!*

Suddenly, I was engulfed by embarrassment. My hands trembled. I pressed down hard on the accelerator and flew out of there. I felt low, very low—almost disgusted with myself. I felt like I could never look Sanjay in the eye again.

On reaching home, I lovingly gifted the book to my

daughter. I had even bought a DVD of a recent movie for my wife from a local store. Sangini was fond of movies, and we had missed that one at the cinemas because of my busy schedule. So that evening, we watched it together, and later I even read out from the book to my daughter. The whole evening was beautiful, and it uplifted my spirits. At night, I slept with a clear conscience, even though my love and desire for Tamanna were as great as ever.

The first thought I had when I woke up the next morning was: *Today, I am going to see Tamanna.* I breezed through my morning routine, counting hours and minutes until she would come in through the door and sit down in our drawing room, as pretty as ever.

At the breakfast table, Sangini was busy on what seemed like an important call. I asked her at what time were Sanjay and Tamanna expected. In response, her eyes widened and her tongue shot out. I immediately knew that she had not made the call. Something tumbled down inside my stomach. I could not bear the thought of not seeing Tamanna for another day. Sangini pleaded through gestures that I call up Sanjay.

Bloody hell!

I went outside to place the call. I detested Sanjay, but now had to sweetly request him to come to our place for dinner. Oh, how I hated the task, how angry I was at Sangini for forgetting to call. The situation reminded me of Mr. Narang.

Mr. Narang was the father of my first girlfriend, Sonia. Before we started dating, I had gone out of my way to impress him, so that there was no resistance from his side later on. I would smile and say hello to him every time I met him in the streets, I helped him with the grocery bags, and even with washing his car!

But that was in 1987. Now, more than twenty years later, I

was doing the same thing with Sanjay. The only difference was that Sanjay was not Tamanna's father.

After deliberating for a minute, I dialled his number. He didn't pick up. *What the fuck!* I dialled again. This time, he picked up after only two rings.

"Hello?"

"Hey, Sanjay. How are you?" I pretended to be excited.

"I am the best." This was his standard response to the question. "How come you are calling me on a Saturday morning? No work?"

Rude was Sanjay's second name. Trying hard to calm myself, I said, "No, *yaar*, I am going to office. Just wanted to enquire if you guys would like to come over for dinner in the evening. Sangini and I—"

"No, man," he interrupted. "We are going to this new pub in CP with an ex-colleague of mine."

FUCK! Do something!

"Ooh, come on, buddy. It's been a long time since the four of us sat together to sip wine and hear your delightful stories. We miss you." I was speaking like an actor speaks his line in a play—sounding convincing but not meaning it. Anything for Tamanna's sake!

"No, Arjun. Today won't be possible. Let's plan for some other day."

You useless fellow! Why are you keeping Tamanna away from me, you moron? You have no respect for her, but she means a lot to me. Why don't you leave Tamanna alone and go away to some different planet?

"Sanjay, you are coming tonight to our place. You know how I am, I will not take a no from you."

"Okay, we will come, but on one condition."

"Whatever, man. Just say it."

"We eat butter chicken prepared by Sangini."

"Sure, man! No problem," I said. "I will ask Sangini to make butter chicken. Anything else?"

"If we could get Heineken . . ."

Bastard! "Haha, yeah, why not?"

"Great, man, I will see you in the evening then."

"See you. Bye!"

I should have been ashamed of myself after the call, but instead, I was elated. Excitedly, I walked back inside and gave Sangini the good news. She readily agreed to make butter chicken. I told her I'd get beer on my way back from office.

The entire day, I kept checking my watch. Each hour seemed like torture. I tried concentrating on work, but to no avail. My heart beat hard inside my chest continuously. Finally, when I could stand it no more, I left office, earlier than usual. First, I drove to a liquor store to buy beer and wine, then to an ice cream parlour for a brick of chocolate chip ice cream, then finally to my home.

As I opened the front door, the smell of butter chicken hit me. I ran to the kitchen to embrace my wife and taste the chicken. It was delicious. I helped Sangini clear up the drawing room, spent some time with Sanghmitra, and finally sat down in front of the TV to await Tamanna's arrival. More than the TV, I watched the clock above it.

When I heard the sound of a car coming to a halt in front of the house, I had goosebumps. My excitement level was unparalleled; my happiness beyond limits. Some seconds later, the doorbell rang. Today it sounded like a romantic song. I ran to open the door.

Sanjay was standing outside. Alone. I felt myself shrinking, deflating.

Whaaaatt??? W-w-where is she . . . WHERE IS SHE?

12

Despite myself, I managed to smile and greet Sanjay. He came in as if everything was normal, not saying anything about Tamanna's absence. Within a single second, a thousand thoughts crossed my mind.

Did they break up? Is she not well? Did she have to go somewhere else? Did she tell him she loved me? Did she run away? Did he kill her?

I was going mad.

Silently, he sat down on the sofa. Sangini came out of the kitchen, greeted him, and asked about Tamanna.

"She will be here in ten-fifteen minutes. She wanted to buy some household stuff from that store down the road."

I felt like I had a won a jackpot. I exhaled an enormous sigh of relief. She would arrive in another ten minutes. Unfortunately Sanjay noticed my relief. He looked at me and commented, "Hey, aren't you happy to see me?"

"No, man, nothing like that," I said. "I have been missing you."

"Let's begin the party then, huh?"

I cursed under my breath and went inside to get the bastard his alcohol. Once we started drinking, he launched into a story of his college days when he had a drinking match with his roommate. He obviously had won the match. His roommate, however, had to be rushed to the hospital. We had heard the story at least thrice already.

Twenty minutes passed. Still no sign of Tamanna.

Another ten minutes passed. Nothing.

Five minutes more. Now it was getting too much.

Where are you, Tamanna? This is not done! I am not going to talk to you. How can you do this? I am very, very angry with you!

Fifty more minutes passed. Sangini was serving snacks to Sanjay—cheese cutlets and French fries.

Idiot! Vermin! Instead of sitting here like a pig and eating all this, go out and bring your wife. Get out, you son of a bitch! Bring her. You have no idea how much I've missed her. Go out! Bring her, pleeeeease!

An hour passed. Neither Sangini nor Sanjay had said anything about Tamanna yet. Unconsciously, I started humming George Michael's "Last Christmas."

Last Christmas I gave you my heart,
But the very next day you gave it away.

Sanjay was boasting about how he used to be the big boss of all his friends in his teenage years. Sangini was smiling and nodding at him.

You worthless baaastardddd! Caaaaallll your wife now! Now . . . right now . . . nowwwwww!

Just then the door bell rang. I sprang up from the sofa and flew to it. It was only while I was opening it that I realised I should have been more careful. By rushing like that, I had probably made Sangini and Sanjay suspicious. Maybe it was all the beer I had consumed.

The next second, all thought was driven out of my mind. Tamanna was standing in front of me. She wore a wonderfully fitted pair of black jeans with a short yellow top that ended just above her belt. Just like Sangini, she too used little or no make-up. Today, her hair was open and even though she looked a bit lost and tired—probably because of the last-minute shopping—the sight of her face was like the sight of heavens for me.

"Hi! Where were you all the while?" the words shot out of my mouth. My tone was one of relief and accusation. "I . . . I mean, we were waiting for you since so long!" I was too happy and excited to check myself.

Tamanna looked startled. She leaned back slightly and said, "Hi, sorry, I was, umm, looking for dresses. I—"

"Hey!" Sangini joined us just then.

Thank God! I had surprised Tamanna already, it seemed.

"Hey, Sangini." Sangini pulled Tamanna inside. "Sorry, I got late!" Tamanna said as they walked in, leaving me alone. I closed the door and followed them.

"Dude, it seems you are exceptionally happy to meet my wife," Sanjay said as I stepped inside. He was clearly tipsy. Then he turned to Sangini. "Isn't he too happy to meet my wife? I expect the same attitude when he meets me!"

His tone was jovial but his intention was clear. Awkwardness descended over the room. I lost my cool and took him to task.

"Sanjay, I don't entertain such cheap remarks. You may not have been concerned about why Tamanna was late, but I was. It has gotten dark and we all know how unsafe Delhi is. She's my friend and I am only relieved to know she is okay and here finally."

There was a shocked silence. Sanjay was glaring at me, while Sangini's eyes were downcast.

Tamanna tried to save the moment. She turned to Sanjay and, with superficial anger, scolded him. "How many times have I told you? Not everyone understands when you joke. One day you will be in trouble because of this."

The pig smiled at his wife. "She is right. I was just kidding, *yaar*."

Chameleon! Liar!

Tamanna turned to me, concerned. "He has a habit of making wrong statements, Arjun. Please ignore him."

But Sanjay's eyes were on me, and they clearly said that Tamanna was only trying to neutralise the situation, that she didn't really mean what she was saying. My temper flared up.

"He should reserve his stupid remarks for his other friends. I like people who talk sensibly," I said curtly.

Tamanna looked towards my wife for help to save the situation.

"Oh, Arjun, you have a habit of noticing too much," Sangini spoke up. "He never meant that. Isn't it, Sanjay?"

"Never," Sanjay said. He never apologised.

Arjun, calm down! I told myself. *He is Tamanna's husband. Don't screw up. If this becomes ugly, you may not get to see her again!*

So I nodded and said, "I'm sorry, I overreacted," and sat down. There were some quiet, tense moments. Then, probably to diffuse the tension, Sanjay said, "Dude, my glass is empty. Can I have some more beer?"

"Sure," I said and went inside to fetch the bastard some more beer.

The rest of the evening, he behaved himself. He didn't play his old records and let the conversation move to more meaningful subjects. He talked less and when he spoke, it was more sensible than usual.

This was a welcome change, but I still didn't enjoy the evening. In fact, I had a really troubling time. The reason? Tamanna was on guard the whole time. She avoided eye contact with me, and whenever she spoke, she looked at either her husband or my wife. She acted the way she'd acted at the beginning of our acquaintanceship two years ago.

After our two meetings and phone calls, I had thought the gap between us had been bridged, and there was no need for that stupid "guard." I'd thought we had become friends.

Maybe she was doing it just to please her husband and convince him that there was nothing going on between her and me (which was true). But her behaviour was hurting me, and hurting badly.

Even while she was leaving with Sanjay, she said only a cold, cosmetic bye to me. Sangini, she hugged. And I had to hug Sanjay to make sure there were no leftover bad feelings. Earlier that evening, I had realised that he was my ticket to Tamanna. Without him, she would be totally gone from my life.

After they left, Sangini asked me if I was okay and called Sanjay an "idiotic pig." Not once did she doubt me. My behaviour could have made her suspicious too. But my wife had complete faith in me. That would have made me guiltier, but I was too bugged by Tamanna's cold attitude towards me.

Am I expecting too much from her? I wondered.

That night I could barely sleep. The next night too, I lay awake till late. So when Monday morning came, it found me very tired. I felt very low too, because I didn't know when I would be seeing Tamanna next. It all depended on when Sanjay invited us for dinner. After the incident on Saturday, I couldn't offer another invitation anytime soon. Neither could I expect Sanjay to invite us for a long time.

Already, I was missing Tamanna a lot.

Before I left for office, Sangini came to my room with her favourite T-shirt and ordered me to fix it. The seams at its armpits had come off and Sangini wanted to wear it to a neighbourhood kitty party. All the stitching jobs in our house were my responsibility. I had learnt *silai-kadai* as a child from

110

my mother and was pretty good at it. Most wives I knew could never order their husbands to stitch their T-shirts, and most husbands would never do any such task for their wives. I enjoyed every bit of stitching it, did it lovingly, attentively and very carefully. I had to make great efforts to match the original just for my darling wife.

On such occasions Sangini's attitude would be that of a small child, the one who would always take his/her parents for granted; one who would never even care to say a small 'thanks'. In our marriage she had shown great dependence on me for many things, and I was gladly ready to give my love and support.

In many ways ours' was a 'one in a million' relationship.

My marriage with Sangini was more equal. We were best friends and each other's life partners. Our roles in the domestic space were not fixed. So lovingly, I fixed the T-shirt for my wife. I enjoyed every bit of it. I did it lovingly, attentively, and very carefully. When I handed it back to her, she didn't say thanks—not because she was not grateful, but because she knew that she didn't need to communicate that to me. We understood each other in such situations without having to speak anything. I knew she was grateful, and she knew I knew that, and I knew that she knew that I knew that, and so on!

On my way to office, I took a detour again in order to pass by Tamanna's house. It had almost become my habit. But, like most days, I could not catch a glimpse of her.

Just wanted to see her once . . . How do I see her? Want to see her once!

I accelerated towards the office, hoping to spend some extra time looking at Deepika's poster. I parked my car and jumped out and got the shock of my life.

Oh my God! No . . . No. This can't happen.

The poster had been removed. Deepika had been replaced

by Aishwarya. I thought I might have a mental breakdown. Whom to ask? Where to go?

Noooooooo!

I was aghast. My throat was choked. I felt as if I was standing at a railway station, in some unknown city, and all my baggage and money had been stolen. I howled and cried within my heart. *Ooohhh God! Please don't do this. I won't be able to take this.*

Using the choicest of abuses, I cursed the advertising companies for their irresponsible attitude. How could they remove posters without any intimation!

With a very heavy heart and tears in my eyes, I looked away and started walking towards my office. Just then my cell phone buzzed. Another nonsensical SMS from Happy: *Raise your voice; come out of the shell. Don't remain deprived. The best sex toys available at WHOLESALE rates. Don't wait but CLAIM TODAY.*

Usually, I would've smiled at its stupidity but at that time, the message had zero effect on me. The only purpose it served was reminding me of Happy. Without thinking, I dialled his number and told him about everything—from the Saturday incident to Deepika's poster.

Happy heard everything patiently and held Sanjay solely responsible for Tamanna's change of behaviour. That brought relief to my heart. He advised, "Listen, dude, don't be emotional. You got to play your cards smartly. You must give Sanjay importance. Don't piss him off. Remember, he is your best man. Lick his ass and you would be happy! In fact, you know what, you should call him up right now and thank him for being a part of last Saturday's dinner. Why, invite him again to your place this weekend! Don't worry about the expenditure, I will pay for the booze if you want."

Wow! As usual, Happy had given me some sound advice,

even though the way he had put it was partially offensive. I loved his idea of calling up Sanjay.

As I looked for the pig's number, my mind again went to Mr. Narang. Twenty years later, I was still impressing the guardian of the girlfriend!

Fortunately, Sanjay didn't mention anything about the Saturday incident when I thanked him for coming. He sounded absolutely fine. So I quickly invited him for another dinner. He probably smelled free beer and readily agreed.

"Any contributions from my side?" he asked, in a rather formal way.

Please, I beg you with folded hands, I bow down my head and request you, please don't forget to bring your wife. Everything is for her! This invitation is for her! Nobody cares whether you come or not. Just bring my Tamanna to me.

While saying all this in my mind, I had forgotten to reply to Sanjay's question. There was silence on the line for a couple of seconds. Then, Sanjay checked, "Hello? Are you there, dude?"

"Oh yes," I fumbled. "No, nothing needed from your side. Your presence is more than enough."

We bid our goodbyes and disconnected. The world had suddenly become a better and brighter place to live in. All my unhappiness at the removal of Deepika's poster vanished. The certainty of seeing Tamanna again the coming weekend supplied much-needed respite to my famished heart. *Eighty hours more*, I calculated, *and Tamanna would be at my place for more than three hours again*. Nobody could stop that from happening now.

Just then it struck me: how to tell Sangini about it all? Won't she find it weird that I had again invited Sanjay to our place, especially after the incident? I wondered how to break this news to her. There had to be a valid explanation. After brainstorming for some moments, I had an idea: I would say that I had called Sanjay to say thanks for coming over on Saturday. During the course of the conversation he had invited us for dinner. Then, just to be polite, I had invited him again, never thinking he would accept it. But the son of a bitch had readily agreed to come. Not only that, he had ordered more beer and butter chicken.

The plan worked. Sangini was easily convinced. She agreed to the dinner without asking too many questions.

So, finally, everything was in place. The day had started out terribly, but a sudden turn of events had put everything back in its place, making me happy—very, very happy. I entered my office—almost an hour late!—with a big smile on my face.

Babbu looked at me with concern as I entered. "Are you okay?" he asked.

"Yes, man. Why, what happened?"

"They, er, removed the poster. Didn't you see?"

"Yeah, I saw. But it's okay, man. I mean, some day or the other, they had to remove it."

Babbu first looked surprised, then disgusted. Then, hopelessly, he shook his head and went back to work.

That afternoon, we had a client meeting in the other side of the city. The long drive and the fruitless meeting were exhausting. By the time we returned to office, after a heavy, oily lunch in Chandni Chowk, I was so sleepy I could barely keep my eyes open. That was not surprising: I had not slept properly for two nights in a row. That day, to keep myself awake, I could not even go to Baskin Robbins and stare at Deepika's poster. So I settled into my comfortable revolving chair and kept my head on my desk. Babbu was outside with our software developer, so the cabin was quiet. In no time, I was in the deepest throes of sleep.

"This is based on my teenage years. I like this story," I said.

"I know," Tamanna said. "But don't create what only you want. Instead, create something for your readers. Think about them. Create something *they* would like." She was standing in front of me, in my office cabin. I was still sitting lethargically in my chair.

"But I *really* like this new story."

She moved closer and sat down on her knees. Affectionately, she took my hands in her own and looked deep into my eyes. "It's been ages since you started writing that rough draft, and it's still incomplete. Do you really think you want to write this story?"

I didn't move, didn't speak. I kept staring at her, as if in a state of hypnosis. Her eyes were oozing compassion and concern. And *love*.

"Arjun, be hundred percent sure of whatever you do. Look deep into yourself and do what your heart says."

"*Ullu ke patthe*! Get up!" Babbu's voice came to me as if from a well. I tried to ignore it and concentrate on what Tamanna was saying.

"SON OF A BITCH!" This time it was a blast in my ear. I jumped up from my chair and almost fell down. Babbu started laughing and walked out. The bastard had come into the cabin only to collect some papers.

"Asshole," I cursed under my breath.

It was such a beautiful dream, so powerful and real! I felt hungover, intoxicated. Tamanna's voice was still echoing in my ears.

I am missing Tamanna. I am, I really am. I must talk to her, she will help me. She will guide me.

My rationality went for a toss. I felt weak and vulnerable and sick.

For the second time that day, I dialled a number without thinking.

The bell was ringing. My mind was blank

"Arjun? Hi!"

Tamanna's voice jolted me out of the hangover instantly.

Gosh! What have you done, you idiot!

I thought of disconnecting the call without saying anything, but then decided against it. It was too late for damage control.

"Hey . . ." I managed to say.

What next? Why have you called!

There was an odd pause right at the beginning! Then, thank God, Tamanna spoke up, "Arjun . . ." she sounded apologetic, "it's so strange. You know, I was just thinking of calling you."

WHAT?! Seriously? "Arjun, uhmmm, I am really sorry about that day."

Yeah . . . yesssss . . . yes!

"No, no, it's okay," I immediately responded.

"No. I know you must have felt bad . . ."

She knows how I felt. Our hearts are aligned together! Tamanna and Arjun belong with each other.

Babbu was at the cabin door. I gestured him to stay outside. The jerk grinned mischievously and went away.

"You know there's a reason why I had to behave like that." She hesitated. "Umm, actually Sanjay doesn't like it . . ."

What? Is she bitching about her husband? Is this call for real? Or am I still dreaming?

"Are you listening, Arjun?"

"Yes, yes, I am here only. You were saying . . . Sanjay doesn't like what?"

Tell me you hate your husband and I will rescue you from that son of a bitch.

"My talking with other men. It becomes so awkward

116

sometimes . . . I wouldn't have told you, I haven't told any of his friends, but then you are not like the others. Unlike you, most of his friends are with him because of some selfish motive."

Slowly and steadily, I was climbing the stairs to the seventh heaven. Keep talking, Tamanna . . .

"You must be wondering why I am telling you such a thing . . ."

"I . . ." I didn't know what to say. *Are you going to tell me you love me too?*

"There is always a reason, no?"

"Yeah . . ."

"Okay, I will tell you. See, Sanjay doesn't have many friends, and whatever friendships he has are of pure convenience. He is a nice man, my husband, but he doesn't understand the meaning of friendship. You can blame it on his upbringing, or to his family structure, but the fact remains that he has a limited understanding of how friends should be. I don't care much about his other friends, but you . . . Sanjay needs a person like you in his life. Though today he might not be able to understand your importance, one day, he will."

I was speechless. My hands were trembling.

Is this for real? Or am I dreaming?

"I don't know what to say," I said truthfully.

"Don't say anything. I just wanted to apologise for the incident on Saturday. Because of his foolishness, Sanjay might lose a great friend like you . . . and I would hate it if that happens."

It was like I had won the Nobel Prize. No, it was like I had won both the Nobel and the Booker!

"So, forgive us, please. We are—"

"Don't be absurd, Tamanna," I finally found the right words. "I am always going to be friends with Sanjay and . . . you."

A pause. "Thanks, Arjun."

"Thanks, Tamanna."

We were inching towards the end of the conversation. Neither of us spoke anything for the next couple of moments.

Say something or this call will be terminated!

I couldn't let that happen. I decided to open up to Tamanna now that she had shared some personal stuff with me.

I shared all my confusion about my book with the love of my life. I told her everything about the story that I had in mind and the doubts I had regarding it.

Tamanna listened to everything with utmost interest. Then what happened shook me to the core. It strengthened my belief in a higher power. Tamanna gave me the same advice the dream Tamanna had given me. At the end she said, "Arjun, whatever you do, give your hundred percent. Listen to your heart. Whatever it tells you is often the truth." These were almost the same words the Tamanna of my dream had spoken.

"You are a gifted writer, Arjun," she continued. "I hope you will become an acclaimed best-selling author one day."

13

The following Wednesday, as I entered home after a hard at work, I had an idea. I switched on my mobile video camera and started recording. I wanted to capture what it was generally like when I returned home from office in the evening.

Like most days, I found Sanghmitra doing her homework with Sangini beside her. The sight of my two dolls cheered and refreshed me up at once. Aware that such beautiful moments were as temporary as morning dew, that time was going to change everything, that we were all going to grow up and lose this innocence, I recorded the lovely scene without pausing.

"How are my kiddos this evening?" I greeted them.

A smile lit up both my girls' faces. "Papa, I am not a kiddo anymore!" Sanghmitra complained. She eagerly waited for me to come back home every evening, I knew.

I took her in my lap. "Oh, so my princess has grown up, huh?" I kissed her on the forehead.

"How was the day?" Sangini asked.

"It was good," I said and pinched her cheek.

God, I love both of them so much. My life is for them. I must give them happiness, comfort, and security.

As I spent those moments with my loved ones, I

could also visualise Tamanna's face without any feeling of guilt or shame.

Every day, after dinner, we ate fruits. But that day, Sangini said she didn't feel like having any fruits. I knew that it was not true, that she was saying that because there were not enough fruits for the three of us. So I ate fewer mangoes than usual and left some for her. When she saw that, she forgot what she'd said and ate the remaining mangoes heartily. Seeing her eat filled my stomach.

That night, after both my princesses had slept, I sat down to read a book by a Buddhist philosopher. The book advised one to follow one's heart no matter what. According to it, the greatest gift a man could give himself was fulfilling his dreams. It was an interesting and meaningful text, but soon after midnight, lethargy overcame my senses, and I fell asleep with the book on my chest and with the bedside lamp on.

"Arjun, Arjun!" It was Sangini, trying to wake me up. "Babbu called up to say that the regional education officer is coming to the office at ten. Wake up!"

I turned around and opened my eyes. It was 9.12 a.m.

"After a long time you have slept for so long." She was right. I was an early morning man. Usually, I woke up at 7 a.m.

"Shit, we have been asking this officer for a meeting for two months!" I jumped up from the bed and ran to the bathroom.

In the shower, I kept wondering how I had slept more than usual.

Then, suddenly, it all came back to me. I had a faint recollection of getting up around three in the night and typing something on my phone.

Was that a dream? I wondered.

It didn't appear like one. I could remember it a little too clearly now. While typing, I had been insane with the desire of meeting Tamanna. I had whispered constantly, "This is for you, Tamanna, this is for you . . . This is for . . ."

Immediately, I turned off the shower and came out of the bathroom. I didn't care that I was not wearing any clothes and that water was dripping from my body. I picked up my phone from the bedside table and opened up the Message folder to see if I had typed any messages. There was nothing. Then I opened the Notes app, an application I used throughout the day to note down my thoughts and ideas and things-to-do. It was there that I found it—a new entry, created at 3.07 a.m. When I opened it, I couldn't believe what I had done.

I had written a poem.

All my life, I had never cared to read or write verse in any form, but in the middle of the night, I had composed a poem, that too one full of love and passion!

I saw you today after a long time.
We suddenly bumped into each other after a long time.
I don't want to see you.
I don't want to be with you.
I can't stand being in front of you.
I can't tolerate being near you.
When encountered with these moments,
I think twice, thrice, and many times.
What excuse should I make? I wonder every time.
No, I don't hate you.
For I can never even think that.
I love you, and this is my fear.
I love you, and this scares me every time.
Oh I love you so much I can't tell you.
When I saw you today, came the rushing desire.
I wanted to hold your hand and run away.

Wanted to hug you tightly and fly.
I saw you and I smiled.
Oh I want to embrace you, but have to stay away.
Oh I want to hold your hand and take you away.
I wait with a bated breath for that moment,
For it will come surely.
But in the next life.
Then I will hold you, embrace you.
Will lift you in my arms and run away.
Until then I will do what I do each day.
Avoid seeing you, for I can't control this feeling.
Avoid seeing you, for I can't be away from you.
Avoid you, for I have no right to be with you.
Avoid you, for I must keep within my limits.
Avoid you . . . for you are not mine.
Until that moment in our next life,
I will keep loving you. Now and forever.
Love you, and love you more, dear Tamanna.

OH MY GOD!

I couldn't believe it. Had I written this myself? How was it possible? I didn't remember writing it at all!

All through my life, my conscious mind had not appreciated poetry, but where my conscience found limitations, my inner instincts, my sub-conscious came alive. That day I found another dimension of my love for Tamanna. My higher conscious had validated it.

"Arjun, breakfast?" Sangini called from the kitchen.

"Uh . . . yes . . . coming!" Suddenly I recalled I was getting late for the meeting. I put all my thoughts regarding the poem aside and got dressed. After a quick breakfast, I ran out of the house. On the way, I took my usual detour towards Tamanna's house, even though I was already ten minutes late. Tamanna, as usual, was not on the balcony, but as I passed her home, I whispered, "I love you . . . I love you . . . I love youuuuu!"

On reaching the office complex, I swiftly parked the car and got out. It was already 10.23 a.m. Hoping that I had not gotten too late, I rocketed to the office. Panting and apologising, I pushed open the cabin door and found Babbu alone inside. He was sitting in my chair, grinning from ear to ear. I was taken aback.

"Did he leave already?" I asked. "Why are you so happy? Was it a successful meeting?"

Babbu got up and hugged me tightly. He was brimming with joy. *We must have gotten a big deal*, I thought.

"I found Simmi!" he blurted out. His eyes, no, his whole face was shining, as if he was radiating vibes of happiness.

"Whaaaat? How? When? Where? Whoaaa!"

Babbu told me the whole story. He hadn't found Simmi-Simmi, but he'd found a classmate named Ranjan who was still in touch with her. Unwilling to reveal his interest in Simmi, he had not asked him any questions about her.

"Now it is your responsibility to call Ranjan to get all the details, including Simmi's number." This was Desperate Babbu's foolproof plan.

"No way! I hardly knew him, man, I am not calling him up."

"Did I ask you a question? I said, 'It is your *responsibility* to call up Ranjan.'" Babbu grinned wickedly.

I had no argument against that. "Okay, I will call him up. But first tell me what happened in the meeting."

"What meeting?"

"The meeting with the regional officer!"

"Oh that? Dumbo, I made that up to bring you here asap."

"You asshole!"

"But that man did call up yesterday. He has promised two schools."

"That is good news!"

"Yes, it is. Now don't waste time. Here's the number. Call Ranjan up."

So I did. I had only vague memories of the guy. I didn't remember ever talking to him properly when we were in school. But, today, I was going to talk to him about the old memories of our student days, the memories I'd never shared with him. For the next half-hour, he was going to become my best buddy. All for the sake of my actual best buddy!

"Hi Ranjan!" I started.

"Who's that?"

"It's me, Arjun!" I said in an over-friendly tone. "Remember me?"

"Arjun Singh?"

"Yes!"

"Oh how could I forget you?" he sounded very excited. "Long time, man! Babbu gave you my number?"

"Yes, he did. Where were you all these years? You never tried to meet your old school friends even once? We shared such kickass years together at school. You forgot all that? I am really, really angry with you."

"Sorry, man." Ranjan's tone was very apologetic. "I have missed you, mate. I thought about calling you a couple of time but then I thought you may not remember me."

"That is bullshit! I clearly remember you. We went on that school trip to Udaipur, remember?"

"Umm, I didn't go on that trip . . ."

Fuck! Ninety percent of the class went on that trip!

"Oh yes, I remember. We missed you, there, man. But leave

all that. So, how is everyone in your family? How are other things? What are you doing in life?"

Ranjan told me everything in great detail. Somehow, he was delighted to get a call from me. Meanwhile, Babbu sat still in his chair, his eyes closed. I wondered whether he was praying for the success of the task he had given me or imagining how it would be like to have sex with Simmi.

"So are you in touch with anyone from school?"

"No . . ."

"No? Nobody? Ravi? Mamta? Sakshi?"

"No, man."

"Seriously? Not even Kamal, Rajesh, Simmi, Neena?"

"No."

Wooosh! I fumbled and went blank. *Had Babbu played a prank on me?* I looked at him. He was staring at me with hope and sex in his eyes.

"Oh wait," Ranjan spoke up. "You confused me with so many names, man. I am in touch with Simmi."

"Oh, that's great! I haven't spoken to her either. You two are alike. No calls, nothing. All old friends forgotten. Do you have her number? I will scold her too for remaining out of touch."

"Sorry, Arjun, I ca—"

"No, I won't take a no from you. Give me her number, and I will greet her with the most innovative abuses."

"Listen, Arjun, she is married. She even has a son."

It was as I had expected. For a moment, I thought of abandoning the topic, but then I looked at Babbu. He was looking like an old man who was about to get his pension with all the dues after waiting for twenty years.

"So what?" I said, angrily. "Am I not married? Don't I have a family, a child? How can you think like that?"

"Oh, I didn't mean that, *yaar*. I . . ."

I am getting tired. Give me her number, damn you!

"Okay, Arjun, here's her phone number."

I signalled Babbu for a pen and paper. He already had a pen with him with its cap off. Instead of paper, he produced his palm, and I wrote down the ten golden digits that made up Simmi's number on it.

I spoke about this and that for a minute more with my new best friend and then excused myself, saying there was a call waiting.

As soon I disconnected, Babbu walked up to me full of emotions and planted a sloppy kiss on my forehead.

"Yuckk!"

"Thanks, man. You are the best. I owe you one."

"You don't owe me anything. But please listen to what happened today morning."

I told him everything and showed him the poem too. I knew he was the wrong person to share this with, but I was hoping he'd surprise me.

"Wow, you are going great guns man!" That was all he said. Too eager to reopen the unfinished chapter of his school days, he flew out of the cabin, clutching his phone in his hand.

I was left alone in the cabin to ponder. What response would he get from Simmi after all these years? Would she even remember him? Or would she still be crazy for him? Would this end in sex? If yes, wouldn't it be wrong? Wouldn't they be cheating on their respective spouses? But then, wasn't I doing the same thing with Sangini? Though there was a difference between Babbu's and my desire—he was driven by pure lust and I was driven by pure love—was it really all that different at the end of the day?

Just then, Tamanna's face flashed before my eyes and

I whispered her name. Then a thought came to my mind: Something that brings me so much happiness couldn't be wrong, could it? Another thought followed it: If it is so right, why can't I disclose it to Sangini, Tamanna, or Sanjay?

I was hopelessly confused. Only one thing was clear: I loved Sangini and Tamanna equally.

14

The same day, around 6 p.m., Happy gave us a surprise. He reached our office with crates of beer and gave a huge, warm hug to Babbu.

"You son of a bitch! You found her after all!" he said and patted his back.

We stacked the beer cans in our small office refrigerator and gave our staff an early off. The first toast was to "Simmi Bhabhi."

"I am so happy. Now both my friends will be settled," Happy said before gulping down half his can.

Settled! I could have clarified that both his friends were already settled, but I didn't want to spoil the fun.

"*Aankhon mein teri ajab si ajab si adaayein hain,*" Babbu was singing in his hopeless voice. It was a beautiful, romantic song, but did not suit Babbu's personality. He had a reason to sing it, however: Simmi had spoken nicely to him. She had sounded excited on hearing his voice after so many years, and when Babbu had hinted at a meeting, she had not been unwilling. After the conversation, he had come back into the cabin in a completely new avatar. Suddenly, he had become soft spoken, well-mannered, and caring, and had called up Happy to share the good news.

During the evening, Tamanna's name was spoken

along with Simmi's many times. Babbu even proposed that we go on a double date soon. I heard everything and laughed along with them and loudly cheered every toast, but it was all pretence. I disliked how they were degrading Tamanna and my love for her by constantly comparing her with Simmi and Babbu's immoral passion for her.

By the end of it, I was irritated. I decided to clarify politely, "Babbu, my darling, do not talk nonsense. Tamanna is not my girlfriend. I love her but that's about it. I don't want to make love to her, neither do I want to go on any dates. You already know all this, don't you?"

"Ohho!" Babbu complained and turned to Happy. Both of them were completely drunk. "The great Arjun, this lover boy, thinks about our bhabhi day and night. He has even written a poem on her. So madly is he in love with her . . . and then he says I do not want to do anything. You are great, Mr. Arjun!"

There was no point explaining anything to my two best friends. So I went out to take a break. I really wanted to be alone for some time. I looked at my cell phone. It was 7:45 p.m. I closed my eyes and tried to visualise what Tamanna must be doing at that moment.

I saw her helping her son with his studies, like Sangini did every evening. From time to time, she went to the kitchen to attend to the dinner.

Is that what you are doing, Tamanna? I whispered and went back in.

We kept drinking and talking till late. The next time I checked my mobile, it was 9.30 p.m. Both Babbu and Happy were five cans down by now. I had finished only two. I was thinking of Sangini. I was missing her, and I knew she must be waiting for me too. She had already called thrice. Each time I had lied that I was in an important meeting.

I had never been one of those husbands who stayed away from home till late to drink with their friends. Instead of going to unwind at bars over drinks, I liked to relax at home with my wife and daughter. But that day I was stuck with Babbu and Happy. I could not leave alone, because both my friends were too drunk to drive back home.

Sanghmitra would sleep around ten. I might not get a chance to talk to her and wish her good-night. Sangini must have had her dinner by now. Even she must be tired. I may not be able to sit with her before going to bed today . . .

Just then, I received her SMS: *when will u b home?*

In 20 mins, sweetheart, I replied.

Ok, then we'll hv ice cream together. Chocolate brick lying at home.

"Let's go, guys, we have had enough alcohol for one day," I said after Babbu had had six cans and Happy seven.

Both of them protested, but I was firm. I wanted to be home as quickly as possible.

"What happened, man? Are you getting late for sex?" Happy asked.

I ignored him and switched off the lights and locked the office. While moving out, Babbu swayed like an elephant, singing, *"Mere sapno ki raani kab ayegi tu . . ."*

I reached home around 10.40 p.m. "Sanghmitra slept only a while back,", Sangini informed me. "She was waiting for you." I felt horrible. "What took you so long? Don't these clients have their own families?" Sangini yawned.

I didn't respond. Quietly, I caressed my daughter's forehead. "Let's have ice cream?" I asked Sangini.

"First you have your dinner. It's is in the kitchen on that big tray. We will have the ice cream later if I am still awake."

I had had only two beer cans with some salty *bhujia* since lunch. I was hungry, but if I had eaten dinner at that time,

Sangini would have surely slept, and I wouldn't have gotten the chance to enjoy ice cream with her. So I lied, "No. The clients had come for the first time, so we ordered heavy snacks. And you know how full I get if I take snacks in the evening. I have space only for some ice cream."

Sangini was easily convinced. I wasted no time in fetching a bowl full of ice cream from the kitchen. Together, we relished it, and then Sangini went to bed. I stroked her hair for some time. I was no longer hungry. The love contained in the moment had satisfied my appetite.

Without making any noise, I started changing into my nightclothes. Before removing my trousers, I emptied its pockets. I had only my wallet, my phone, and a handkerchief. A feeling of hollowness crept inside me as I looked into my wallet. It contained only 150 rupees. I didn't have much money in the bank either. We had been waiting for some pending payments for a couple of weeks.

I looked at my two dolls. They were sleeping peacefully. I felt empty inside. I closed my eyes and prayed to God to set everything right. After changing, I went to the study room to read. I had barely read one page before my eyes began to droop. I kept the book aside and went to bed. *Good night, Tamanna,* I wished before closing my eyes.

The next morning, I woke up with a heavy heart. I remembered dreaming that Tamanna was at our home, but she was not talking to me. She was totally ignoring me even though I was right in front of her. Even when I called her name, she didn't respond. I was pleading, "Please don't do this, Tamanna! Talk to me! I feel bad, very bad." But she would not listen. Then suddenly I had woken up, sweating. I had looked at my phone to check the time. It had been 4.21 a.m. Then I had . . .

Oh my God! I picked up my cell phone and opened the Notes app. I had created another poem. This one oozed with pain.

The other day, at the family gathering,
You looked weak and tired.
"Don't worry and take rest," I said.
"Eat healthy food," I had to say.
So formal my statement was.
So casual my words were.
If only I could say what I really wanted to.
If only I could do what was there in my heart.
I looked at your face and prayed.
Prayed not for you, but for some silly thing.
God oh God, can't I have magical powers?
To do what my soul really desires.
Can't I have a parallel invisible "me"?
So that I may do what I want and nobody could see.
God oh God, can't it happen this way?
Grant me this wish, so that I may get up,
And hold your hand and say, "Take rest."
Hold your face and say, "Don't worry."
"Come, I'll make you sleep.
I will stroke your hair.
So tired you are,
I'll gently massage your feet.
And I'll cook the finest food for you.
Your tired nerves need relief,
I'll sing a song for you."
I say as loudly as I can
In my heart and through my soul.
God oh God, can't you grant me this magical power?
So that I may give her the comfort of my arms.

So that I may give her the warmth of my love.
Feelings are feelings.
Can never reveal my secrets to you, I know.
Now I am back where I was earlier,
Sitting on the couch in front of you.
Seeing you, watching you, and hiding my feelings.
"Don't worry and take rest," I say again.
The other day we met and I saw you down.
Secretly sending my love to you.
Love you and love you more.

Oh dear, oh my dear, oh dearest Tamanna . . .

It was an average verse but the manner in which I had composed it was like a re-introduction to myself. I was stunned. My mind went blank.

Gosh, what are you up to, Arjun?

Some moments later, I heard Sangini talking to the maid. The day had to start. I got up from the bed and slowly opened the door of the adjacent room. It was empty. Sanghmitra had left for school. I had missed her by five minutes. She left every day at sharp 6.55 am.

Sighing deeply, I sat down on her bed. I caressed her sheet and pillow and whispered, *"It's been more than 24 hours since we spoke properly."*

I felt awful! If only I had woken up 5 minutes earlier . . . My daughter was so thoughtful. She hadn't said bye to me before leaving, for she must not have wanted to wake me up.

"I will go meet her in school with a rose."

Sanghmitra was surprised to see me in school. I hugged her and apologized for not being able to meet her the previous night. Finally I gifted her the rose.

The twinkle in her eyes made my day.

Such was my bond with my daughter that whenever she got hurt while playing, tears would roll down from my eyes. When she would be unwell, I would sit by her side for the whole night. Whenever she complained of stomach ache, I would feel as if my appetite had vanished.

***

Babbu came in wearing a red T-shirt with blue jeans and light-brown shades. The whole day, he kept exchanging messages with Simmi. After lunch, he called her up and they talked for an hour. In the evening, I found him browsing some websites about sex and sexual positions. Many tabs were open on his window: *how to orally satisfy a woman; how to get the 'Big O' in a quicky; how to rub her G-spot correctly; how to stay active and last longer*. He was reading the techniques and advices as religiously as an eighteen-year-old boy preparing for his IIT entrance.

"Just trying to polish my skills, man," he explained.

I sighed and returned to my seat. The two poems I had composed were open on my monitor. I had copied them to my computer from my phone. By now I had read them at least twenty-five times.

Just then, my phone beeped. It was an SMS from Happy.

Hi buddy. Are you game for tomorrow's Love Dinner? Please don't bother to buy any eatables. I will be ready with beer and other drinks. I also have lots of frozen snacks at home. Buddy, this is my party...just don't bother at all...I mean it.

Happy had not forgotten his promise to sponsor the beer. The message was like sudden rain on a hot sultry day. Actually, I had no money to pay for the dinner the next day. I had been worrying about it and was planning to borrow some money from Babbu.

I messaged back: *U jst get d sncks. D drinks r on me.*

Happy's reply came a minute later: *Don't be so formal asshole. I am so happy that Tamanna is coming. I am so happy for you man. So, don't spoil my mood. Both drinks and snacks are on me.*

I could not say no to that. *Ok, mate,* I replied.

I called up Sangini to inform her that the snacks and drinks were on Happy.

"Okay," she said. "I called up Tamanna to remind her about the dinner an hour back. The sweet dish is on her. She is bringing caramel custard. They'll be here by 7.30."

Caramel Custard, I whispered to myself as I disconnected the phone. I sat back in my seat. *How would it taste? The custard, sugar, caramel, everything would be coming from her hands!*

I closed my eyes and tried to visualise the scene. I saw Tamanna standing in her kitchen, mixing the custard powder in milk. She was doing it very carefully. Her beautiful fingers were slowly moving inside the big steel bowl. She was wearing a blue tight-fitted cotton suit, without the dupatta. It suited her picture-perfect figure. She took a spoon and checked the taste. She frowned. The taste had not been as she had expected. She took another spoonful of the mixture. She used the same spoon that had just touched her tongue, her mouth, her saliva.

I opened my eyes and calculated. *Twenty-three hours from now, I would get to taste a dish touched by Tamanna's fingers.*

I could already feel the taste of Tamanna's soft fingers in my mouth. I was salivating.

That dish is mine. God, give it to me. It is mine!

After visualising Tamanna making the caramel custard, I realised I couldn't work. So I left office earlier than usual. On my way out, I hummed the popular *Titanic* song.

Every night in my dreams, I see you, I feel you. That is how I know you go on.

Passersby looked at me weirdly, but I just smiled at all of them. There was a new movie at Satyam Cineplex: *Love Aaj Kal*. Its poster had the lead pair Saif Ali Khan and Deepika Padukone. And again I could see my Tamanna in Deepika. This was like a cherry on the cake, or rather, cherry on the caramel custard!

Just then, I felt my phone vibrate in my pocket. I picked it up without seeing the caller id.

"Hiiii!" I almost sang my greeting.

Somebody giggled softly on the other side.

It is Tamanna, my heart suggested. I was about to take her name, but luck saved me! "What's up, Arjun? Some good news? You sound very happy." It was Sangini.

I was embarrassed. I thanked God for saving me.

"Oh yes, don't you know Sanjay is coming tomorrow?" I replied.

There was a pause. *Fuck, did I say something wrong?* Then Sangini spoke up, "Shouldn't we call some band baja walas too?"

Thank God she didn't get suspicious!

"Oh yes, I will book them tomorrow."

"Oh come on, enough of this poor humour. Seriously now, what happened?"

"Nothing, yaar. It is just that today I worked hard. I am really happy with myself."

"That's good news!" Sangini sounded delighted.

"Yeah . . ." I was starting to feel guilty.

"Hmm, anyway, I called to ask if you've paid this quarter's fees to Sanghmitra's school?"

This question brought me crashing down. I had again delayed the fees payment. There was no money in my bank account.

"Yes, I paid it few days back," I lied.

"Okay, great. Bring one kg paneer on your way back. I will need it for dinner tomorrow."

"Okay, darling."

As I disconnected the call, tears welled up in my eyes. I was ashamed and mad at myself.

You haven't paid your daughter's school fees and you were fantasising about caramel custard? Shame on you.

'There's nothing more unfortunate than seeing a man being unable to support his family financially,' words from a great Buddhist philosopher echoed in my mind.

'Please do something Arjun! Please do something my dear!' I almost pleaded to my own self.

I got into my car and started driving. Hundreds of thoughts were running through my mind, and I was on the verge of breaking down. I drove mechanically, trusting my instinct to take me home.

Sometime later, I found myself at the Mayapuri crossing. There was always a jam at this signal. There were many cars around me, so I took out my handkerchief and wiped off my tears. A moment later, I noticed that someone was standing by my window.

It was a eunuch. I had noticed her several times before, begging at the same signal. The reason she had caught my attention was that unlike other eunuchs at the signal, she looked attractive. Medium height, dusky complexion, and a thin, attractive figure. She carried herself decently and with dignity, quite different from all the other beggars. She would never wait in front of any vehicle or knock on the car window repeatedly. Seeing her, I would wonder how her life was. What had led her here, to this crossing, to begging?

Strangely, she had never begged at my window before.

On all previous occasions, either she would pass my window without stopping or the signal would turn green when she was on her way to my car. But today, finally, she was knocking on my window. She was wearing a chiffon sky-blue sari, small golden earrings, dark maroon lipstick, and a small round bindi that suited her. Her hair was tied in a simple ponytail.

Normally, I never gave alms to beggars, but to this eunuch, I felt like I had to give something. I took out my wallet and chose a twenty-rupee note for her. Then I rolled down the window and respectfully gave it to her.

"Thank you," she said in English and pressed the note to her forehead.

I was about to roll up the window and she was about to turn around when I decided I was going to talk to her. It was a sudden decision. I wanted to know her story and wanted to tell her my story too. I acted on instinct.

I called her out and asked, "Listen, can I, umm, talk to you for a m-minute? Don't-don't . . . get me wrong. I just w-w-want to talk . . . nothing else." I was stammering badly.

"Sir, please cross the signal, I will meet you on the other side," she responded with a friendly smile and walked towards the other side of the huge crossing.

That was not the kind of response and voice I was expecting. I was expecting her to refuse me in a fake-feminine voice. But she had sounded husky; neither masculine nor fake-feminine. I had heard that kind of heavy female voices before.

Now that she had said yes, my pulse quickened. How was I going to talk to her, that too in public?

Nervously, I waited for the signal to turn green. In the side mirror on my right, I saw two men on a bike pointing at me and talking amongst themselves. When the light turned green and I started moving, they shouted, *"Masti karo, bhai, masti karo."*

As the traffic started running, I lost sight of her. I slowed down and began to shift towards the leftmost lane, all the while looking for her. Finally, I spotted her at a distance of about 150 metres from the crossing.

I stopped the car beside her and she gestured to me to roll down the other window. When I did that, she leaned inside and said, "Arjun-ji, I know you."

15

"Don't be so surprised, sir. I saw your book some weeks back."

"Oh . . ." I exhaled.

She smiled. "I must say you surprised me too. A person like you stopping the car for somebody like me . . . people won't take it in the right light. If someone known to you sees you here, it would spoil your reputation."

That was true. But I didn't care about the world, like it had not cared about me when I was down in the dumps for years. "Don't worry about that. I just want to talk to you. Can you, umm, please get in? I will drop you back here in a short while."

She appeared apprehensive, but then she opened the door and elegantly sat down on the front seat.

As I started the car, she began speaking, "I saw you at the crossing last week too. I was very excited to see a writer in reality. *Gross In . . . Injustice*, that's the title of your book, no?"

She had actually read the book! I was still finding it hard to digest that someone like her had read my book.

She told me her name was Jyoti. The name was given to her by her parents, and the group of eunuchs who had taken her in at the age of ten had continued with it. She was born in Bhopal, had stayed in Varanasi till the age of eighteen, and then had lived in Kanpur. She was now twenty-three and had arrived in Delhi only seven months back.

In the capital, her caretaker and group head was Radha Rani, a big name in the eunuch community. Her name sounded familiar to me, but it was only later that I recalled why it was so. Radha Rani was the head of the group of eunuchs who had come to my house to bless Sanghmitra at the time of her birth. She was fifty-five years old and was famous in this part of Delhi. According to Jyoti, Radha Rani was almost like her foster parent. She had been kind to her, and even allowed her to read books occasionally.

When Jyoti's parents had realised who she was—a woman trapped in a man's body—they had wanted to give her away. In their opinion, as long as she was around, her siblings would never have a future. They had sent her to an English medium school till Class 5. After that, they had given her over to a local group of eunuchs and told their neighbours and relatives that their son had run away from home.

At her new house, Jyoti had found more love and acceptance than she had ever found in her parents' home. She was groomed and educated by the seniors. She had always had very little hair on her body and possessed a feminine face and figure.

When she grew old, she learnt about the dark reality of their world. Nobody gave them employment. The society shunned them. All the money they earned was through flesh trade and dancing and offering blessings at big functions and parties. Even though Jyoti attracted more attention than her sisters, she had never sold her body for sex, but she had had to resort to begging in order to survive. Even so, she earned as much money as the others did, and was therefore the apple of Radha Rani's eyes.

A couple of months ago, an NGO had started working in the area where she lived. The organisation had started a night school for the community, where they offered courses like sewing, handicrafts, and cooking—all meant to help the community members find jobs and earn a respectable living. The NGO had also been inviting counsellors and motivational speakers to sensitise the ignored and unfortunate souls about human life and its objectives.

With the support of Radha Rani and the NGO, Jyoti had been able to indulge in her passion for reading and writing. She often borrowed books from the NGO staff and had come across my book one day. Even though her English was very poor, she had sincerely attempted to not only read the book but also understand its nuances. I was absolutely astonished to know this.

After finishing her story, Jyoti glanced at me, probably expecting some response. But I had none. My throat was choked. I felt intensely ashamed of myself. I had been begrudging my life only a short while back, and here was a person whose entire life had been a struggle but who still fought on with more courage than a hundred men put together. My car was now slowly making its way through the interiors of Delhi Cantt. By now, I had forgotten I was sitting in my car with a eunuch I had picked from a red light. I felt completely at ease.

"Uhh . . . you must be wondering why I spoke to you today," I said. "It was very awkward . . . isn't it?"

With a faint smile on her lips, she glanced at me and sighed deeply. "After reading your book I had a desire . . . somewhere in one corner of my heart . . . to meet you. I always thought it was a stupid desire, because it seemed it would never come true." That made me smile. "It was odd, sir, yes, I won't lie. So tell me, why did you want to speak to me?"

Before I could speak up, my cell phone beeped. *Reminding you, plz dont forget to bring paneer.*

I had completely forgotten about Sangini. The SMS reminded me not only about the paneer, but also about the last conversation that I had had with her.

"Don't call me 'sir,'" I said. "I don't deserve any respect. I haven't been able to fulfil any of my responsibilities. I may look like a scholar . . . but I am a complete failure." Somehow, I felt at ease opening up my heart's deepest secrets and insecurities to Jyoti. She had told me her life story and deserved to know my secrets. So I continued. "I could not become a worthy son. I am not a good husband . . . and I am a father who cannot fulfil the whims of his daughter." I blinked back tears.

For the next few moments, both of us remained silent. Jyoti made an attempt to comfort me by touching my shoulder, but didn't do it finally.

"Where should I drop you?" I asked finally.

"I want to be a better and much more successful actress than Aishwarya Rai," Jyoti said suddenly, surprising me. Her tone was resolute and confident; her gaze was fixed on the road ahead. "You must think I am a fool. How can a eunuch ever become Aishwarya Rai? you must wonder. But, no, I never befool myself, sir." She turned towards me. "I narrated my life story in about ten minutes. But do you think everything happened in ten minutes only? The life of a eunuch. How do you think it is? My soul was cut into pieces. The skin of my dignity was ripped apart daily." She was breathing heavily now. "Sir, it is painful . . . very, very painful." She paused. "Sir, maybe I have voluntarily chosen this life. I believe in past birth, so maybe this life is the result of some grave offences done by me in the last life.

"Sir, human life is about 'free will.' We do what we want.

143

We suffer and we rejoice as per our actions. Within my heart, I have ceaselessly prayed to change my circumstances. I've prayed every day for a complete turnaround. But my pain and heart-wrenching situations never stopped. I took it all as part of my karma, my destiny, which I would certainly change. Sir, I sing and people say that I am really good at it, so I spent my earnings to buy a cassette player and records of various singers. Sir, for six years I have been continuously practising, and I will definitely become a better, bigger, and more successful actress than Aishwarya Rai one day.

I smiled at her innocence. She did not know that Aishwarya did not sing her own songs.

"No, sir, I am not joking. See, this life is a big drama itself. Just like a movie, everyone's life comes to an end. In this part, I am performing the role of a eunuch, a eunuch who, despite all adversities, would change her life . . . This role was assigned to me by life itself, and I will do my best to give a memorable performance. This world is a stage, and I have got talent, so I will shine."

I was speechless. My car had reached Kirby place, the exit of Delhi Cantt. "Sir, drop me at Brar square." I nodded. "Sir, not much time is left . . ." she continued. "The NGO working in our area . . . they are the answer to my countless prayers. Even coming to Delhi is an answer to my prayers . . . else I would have stayed and died in Kanpur only. Rekha didi, the head of the NGO, she is impressed by my singing." She chuckled. "She says I can win *Indian Idol*. She had called some musicians to our area two weeks ago . . . they too were of the same opinion."

I stopped the car at Brar Square

Before getting down, Jyoti looked at me intently for some seconds. She was choosing the best words for her conclusion. "Sir, sitting with you is indeed a dream come true for me . . .

In fact this too is the answers to my prayers. Very soon on a big stage, Aishwarya Rai will be congratulating me . . . giving me an award for best performance, for playing the role of a eunuch and coming out completely victorious in life. Sir, soon the world would know me as the greatest performer of life.

"Sir, when I pray, I pray without any doubt. When I read your book, I had a stray desire in my heart . . . a desire that got strengthened over time. A desire to turn the tables, to change everything, to become proud of my life. I prayed that I am able to meet you and request you to write Jyoti's story . . . about her pain and her glorious victory."

I was overwhelmed. "Surely . . . that's my commitment," I responded in a cracked voice. My eyes were moist. My lips were trembling. Jyoti clasped my hands lovingly. "Your biography would be an honour for me," I added.

That brought a huge smile to her face. She stepped out of the car and leaned in through the window again. "Sir, never begrudge your life . . . If wonderful people like you start doing such silly things, then just think of us, people like me.

"Sir, your book is good, it touches the heart . . . but it is full of intense anger. Indeed the world is bad, it is difficult to survive here . . . but, sir, the world is good too. It has got wonderful people too. We cry and we laugh, we sometimes lose, sometimes win . . . The hero of your book, Pawan, he is very nice, very pure, but he can only make people cry . . . I cried too, sir, relating myself to him . . . but, sir, it is my humble request . . . this time do exactly the opposite. Replace all the anger with love."

With that, she walked away.

On my way back home, I felt really inspired. In about forty-five minutes, I had learnt a great lesson of life. I had met Jyoti in a broken state and she had left me with a rock-solid conviction. A fresh lease of life had kissed my soul, and I was now counting all the wonderful blessings of my life—my new profession, writing skills, supporting friends, and, of course, my two princesses.

As I parked my car and got out, two things were going in my mind:

(1) Keep it up, Jyoti, the world is waiting for you.

(2) Shame on you, Arjun. You better never cry again for being a failure in life.

I never saw Jyoti after that day. But she has inspired me ever since.

16

It was 10.50 p.m. The television was on, playing an old Hindi movie that no one was watching. Sangini, on my right, was dozing off now and then. Sanghmitra, on my left, had placed her legs on my thigh and was already asleep. And I was thinking about my revealing encounter with Jyoti.

The beeping of my cell phone brought me out of my reverie. It was kept on the bedside table. Even before I would lean over and pick it up, it beeped again, and again, and again, a total of five times.

Must be promotional messages. Idiots! Who messages at this hour?

The messages were from my network provider. Five missed call alerts. All from the same number—Tamanna's! My heart skipped a beat.

I looked at Sangini. She was fast asleep. The message beeps had not woken her up. I saw the missed call timings. All five were between 7.20 p.m. and 7.35 p.m. At that time, I had been in the car with Jyoti, driving around the high-security Delhi Cantt area where mobile signals were always a problem.

Damn Delhi Cantt and damn Airtel! If Sangini's SMS could reach me, so should have Tamanna's calls. She called five times! Five! Must have been something important.

I could not return the calls now; it was too late. I was so furious with Airtel I wanted to call Sunil Mittal and tell him that due to his company's incompetence, the love of my life had not been able to speak to me about something very urgent.

Quietly, I got up, switched off the TV, and went to the study room. I was so agitated I didn't care to even switch on the lights or the fan. I just sat on the bed and tried to figure out what to do.

Oh God, Tamanna! I am so sorry. Sanjay, my dear Sanjay, would you mind if I call up your wife at this hour? Please, let me call her up, please! It is important. Please. It won't make any difference to you. Tamanna, you could have sent an SMS, couldn't you? At least I would have known the purpose! Sanjay, you bloody bastard, it is because of you that I can't call Tamanna right now!

An hour later, I was still sitting inside the room. By now I had opened the message box of my phone and caressed the five missed-call messages with my thumb at least a hundred times. I was really missing Tamanna. Then an idea struck me.

Why didn't this strike me earlier!

I took out my Acer laptop, switched it on, and hurriedly logged in to Facebook. I was not an active user of the social networking site; I logged in only once in a while and that too only for a couple of minutes. The last time I had logged in was more than a fortnight ago. At that time, I had noticed that I had gotten a friend request from Sanjay. Smirking, I had ignored it. I didn't want the pompous bastard on my friends list. But only now I realised that I had been foolish to do that. By ignoring the request, I had probably ignored a box of treasure for me.

Now, I gladly accepted the request and quickly browsed through his friends list, hoping to find Tamanna. But she was not there. That probably meant she was not on Facebook, otherwise why wouldn't she be added to her husbands' profile?

I was disappointed but not defeated. I went to his photos folder and browsed through it. And it was there that I found my jackpot. Sanjay's account had photographs, lots of them.

You self-obsessed creature! I love you!

Unfortunately, the jackpot was not as big as I had expected. Mostly all the photos were Sanjay's solo shots. Tamanna was present only in ten photos. In six of them, she was more or less lost in a big family crowd. Three showed her with her husband; all of them had Sanjay with his right arm around her. In the left, he held a cigarette. The last one was Tamanna's solo shot. She was standing in front of their home, wearing a black top with red slacks. Her hair tumbled gracefully around her shoulders. Her ravishing figure and pretty face resembled Deepika Padukone's.

I wasted no time in downloading the photo to my computer. Then I switched on the fan, lay down in the middle of the bed with my legs folded and my head on a pillow, and placed the laptop on my thighs. Tamanna's photo was open on the screen. It seemed to have been sent from the love gods themselves. I stared at the photo for a long time, until it was branded into my memory.

Missing someone so badly is such an indescribable condition. With mouth half open, breathing slowly and heavily, eyes looking nowhere but imagining the beloved's face, body stuck and remaining in the same posture and some strange, very strange craving emerging from deep within your heart, probably right from the core of your being—this is what missing badly means. And such was my condition at the time.

I didn't come to know when I slipped peacefully into slumber.

"Arjun? Arjun?" Someone was patting my shoulders and trying to adjust my pillow. "Arjun, sleep properly. Why do you have to work at such odd hours? Come on, lie down properly." Half-asleep, I did as she instructed. "I have kept the laptop on the table. You should be more careful with it. It could have fallen down from the bed."

Her words hit me like a thunderbolt. My eyes flew open. I was fully awake at once. Sangini was pulling the blanket over me. My laptop was resting on the study table; its flap was closed. The wall clock announced it was 1.18 a.m. My heart was beating wildly beneath my shirt.

Fuck, did she see Tamanna all over the screen? I wondered. *Damn you, Arjun! How could you be so careless, you stupid, stupid man!*

I looked at Sangini again. She looked normal. She had probably not seen that her husband had been staring at some other woman's photograph and not working. If she had seen the photograph, she would have surely kicked me awake. But then this was Sangini. You could never be sure what was going on in her mind. Sometimes, she repressed ugly memories, which would then keep rotting inside her, slowly infecting her mind. I decided to check.

Trying my best to sound casual, I asked, "Honey, you didn't close the file I was working on, did you?"

"No, I didn't do anything. By the time I came inside, the laptop had already run out of battery."

I felt the relief of a man who had missed a flying bullet by a few inches. "Okay," I muttered and turned towards the other side. Sangini went out and closed the door behind her.

I kept lying still for some time, my ears trying to pick up any noise, my heart still beating heavily. When I didn't hear anything for a few minutes, I concluded that Sangini had gone back to bed. Quietly, I got up and checked the laptop. It was lifeless. I kissed it near the webcam and thanked Acer from the bottom of my heart. For a moment, I felt a strong desire to switch on the laptop again and see Tamanna's photo once more. But, sensibly, I curbed this desire and went back to bed.

I woke up earlier than usual, around 6 a.m. The first thing I did was plugging the charger into my laptop and seeing Tamanna's picture once. After satiating my eyes for a few moments, I closed the window and shut down the laptop. When that was done, I walked to the bedroom, feeling uneasy and disturbed and confused and ashamed.

I found my two dolls sleeping soundly in the other room. Without making any noise, I slipped in between them. The movement woke up Sangini. She yawned and murmured, "When did you get up?" Then, without waiting for a reply, she turned to the other side and went back to sleep. I put my head on Sanghmitra's forehead and stroked her hair as softly as possible.

"Papa, I want to sleep more," she said and removed my hand.

I smiled and kissed her forehead and leaned back on my pillow. I looked from my wife to my daughter. *This is my paradise,* I thought.

***

As I got ready for office, I decided to tell Sangini about the Jyoti incident. Last night, I had not told her because I wasn't sure how she'd react. But now, I was feeling guilty about already hiding so much from her. I realised that my doubts about her reaction were unfounded too, because I knew she was the kind of person who would understand my little story and respond kindly.

So, at the breakfast table, I revealed everything to her, except the part about our financial situation. Sangini listened patiently till the end and then gave her verdict.

"Wow, Arjun." She placed her hand on mine. "I am stunned. I wish I was there with you to meet Jyoti in person and listen to her story in her own voice. All this makes one think why we complain all the time about what we don't have, no? There are always millions of others who are worse off than us. Stories like hers put everything in perspective. You should really write it down. I am sure people will love to read it."

"Yeah, you are right," I said.

She smiled. "Okay, you should leave for office now, I guess. It's getting late. I asked Tamanna to come a little early, around 7 p.m. We will try to wind up in time. Otherwise things get very late."

I nodded and got up. Before leaving, I kissed Sangini's forehead. As soon as I sat down in the car, I recalled the five missed calls from Tamanna. I looked at the time.

Baby elephant must be passing his time in school, I thought and dialled Tamanna's number.

After a few beeps, the most undesirable voice in this world said the most unwanted words to me, "The number you are trying to reach is currently switched off. Please try again later."

I tried again thrice within the next two minutes. Each time, the same irritating voice greeted me.

Nooooo. This is wrong . . . wrong! It doesn't happen this way. This is being so irresponsible. What if there was some urgent matter? No way, this is wrong!

Just then, I received a taunting message from Babbu reminding me about an important meeting we had scheduled on Tuesday for that morning: *Sarkar, are you coming for the meeting? Or should I order beer to lure you?*

I had been so lost in calling Tamanna that I had not even started the car. I tried her number once again, but got the same response. Then I turned on the ignition and accelerated towards the office. All through the journey, I kept trying her number.

I hope she has the missed call alert service active. Let her get at least twenty messages when she switches on her phone.

I took the usual detour, but she was nowhere to be seen, yet again. That made me angrier. On reaching Janakpuri, I quickly parked the car. Before getting out, I tried her number one last time. Still switched off!

Huh, I couldn't take calls yesterday because of the signal problem. Now she wants to settle the score.

At the office, the meeting went very well. I kept aside all the mess going on in my head and gave my 100% to the discussions. The outcome was way beyond our expectations. We were going to work with two big South Delhi schools.

When the clients left, Babbu and I ordered cold coffee, and I told him about my encounter with Jyoti. I did not expect him to understand anything. I was just curious to see what the asshole would have to say about the incident.

Throughout my narration, he kept interrupting with, "Oh fuck!", "Oh my God", and "Bencho!"

When I finished, he gave a more elaborate reply: "Arjun *yaar*, frustrations of life have led you to stoop to such low levels." He shook his head. "Have you thought about how Tamanna would feel if she comes to know about this? Did you give that a thought?" Then he took a deep breath. "Tell me honestly, you didn't have sex with this . . . this *woman*?" His face expressed disgust.

I rolled my eyes, sighed, and went back to my seat without responding. Before starting work, I again tried calling Tamanna, but to no avail. I had to speak to her before the dinner because I knew she would not say anything about the calls in front of Sanjay.

Around noon, Babbu's phone rang. He saw the caller id, jumped up, and ran out of the room. I understood it was Simmi's call. I shook my head and again dialled Tamanna's number. Still nothing.

I sighed. I was waiting for some replies from our vendors and had no work to do. So I sat back in my seat and closed my eyes. Tamanna's face flashed before my eyes. I tried to think what could be wrong. Why was her phone switched off since morning?

Then an idea occurred to me: they must have a landline connection too. But I didn't have the number. I tried to figure out a way I could take that number, but could not come up with anything. If I asked either Sangini or Sanjay, they were likely to become suspicious.

Suddenly I was furious at Sanjay. So proudly and arrogantly he was sitting between me and my love.

Sanjay, I imagined speaking to him in my head, *you are most welcome to come to my home. You come, you eat, drink, and boast. Do whatever. It doesn't matter to me. But please, PLEASE, can I talk to Tamanna once? Just once! Can I hear her sweet voice? Tamanna. Your wife. Please, man. Just once . . .*

I looked at my cell phone again and stared at her number in the call log. Even though I was going to meet her in a few hours, I was missing her terribly. The craving to see or talk to her right at that time was maddening. Almost mechanically, I took out my phone, opened the notes tab, and started composing a new message.

The words came to my mind like they had a power of their own. I typed nonstop, creating a verse that expressed what missing someone was like. It was as if a higher power was guiding me. My fingers danced to the command of my heart. When I finished, I found myself breathing heavily, like I had just run a marathon. I was also feeling tremendously relieved, like someone had physically lifted an iron-weight from my stomach.

17

It was 7 p.m. Sangini and I were waiting for Tamanna and Sanjay to arrive. My legs were trembling. I was feeling extremely nervous. At 7.15, the door bell rang.

"I think they are there," Sangini said and got up.

I started shivering. There were goosebumps everywhere on my body. For a second, I thought I'd faint.

How will you face Tamanna like this?

Suddenly, I remembered something my drama teacher had told me in school. He had said that if you are nervous before a performance, you should breathe deeply and try to think of something funny. I decided to employ his technique today.

I let my mind wander and create a funny image. I had very little time to do it; Sangini was already greeting Tamanna outside. The first picture that came to my mind was of Sanjay riding a filthy little pig. Eight more pigs were walking with him, four in front and four behind. Sanjay, full of himself as usual, was repeatedly shouting, "I am the best! I am the best! I am the best!"

Now, it wasn't a very funny image. In normal circumstances, it may not have even made me smile. But at that time, with my nerves on the edge, I thought it was hilarious, and so, when Tamanna and Sanjay entered the living room, they found me laughing like a madman.

They stopped whatever they were talking about and looked at me curiously. I tried to control my laughter, but in vain.

"What happened to you?" Sangini narrowed her eyes.

"Nothing," I managed to say. "Hi, Sanjay. Hi, Tamanna." I was beginning to calm down.

"Hi, dude, what's so funny?" Sanjay asked.

"Nothing, nothing." I had finally stopped laughing.

"Come on, share the joke with us," Tamanna said.

I noticed that both Tamanna and Sangini were wearing almost identical suits. Both were white-coloured and had some pink embroidery on the neckline and sleeves. Only the design of the embroidery and the shade of pink differed. Since their height and figure were the same too, today they looked like two sides of the same coin, each lucky in her own way.

"It's nothing, man. Good to see you both."

"Both? Hmmm, he only feels good when he sees both of us. Hmmm, that means separately I have no importance. Well then, should I go back? Tamanna will stay here," he said and winked at me. He was back to being a pig.

I wanted to punch him then and there and break his teeth, but I only said, "I feel happy seeing both of you, both separately and together."

Sanjay laughed. "Ohhoo! Arjun, why do you always take my comments in the wrong way?"

I looked at Tamanna. She had a cosmetic smile on her face and was avoiding looking at me.

Sangini acted as the saviour. "Oh come on, guys," she said. "You men are all alike; always pulling each other's leg." With that, she suggested we all sit, and when we did, she turned to Tamanna and asked the question I desperately wanted answered. "Why was your phone switched off the whole day? I tried calling a couple of times . . ."

"Oh, I'm so sorry. Actually, we had some unexpected guests and I was on my toes the whole day. I didn't get the time to even charge my phone," Tamanna explained. "Oh, and I also didn't get the time to make the custard. I'm extremely sorry."

"Oh that's absolutely okay. There is a lot of ice cream in the fridge. We will serve that for dessert."

The doorbell rang again and Sangini brought inside Happy this time. He was carrying a huge bag with him. It had Kingfisher beer, Bacardi breezers, and red wine. It was too much. I had told him to get only beer. He asked Sangini to place everything in the refrigerator and greeted all of us.

Sanjay turned to me. "*Yaar* Arjun, you should have told me too. I could have also contributed."

Before I could politely respond, Happy spoke up, "Oh that's okay, buddy. Next time, the drinks will be your baby entirely."

We all laughed. Sangini got up to get snacks for everyone. Tamanna stood up too to help her, but Happy stopped her. "You sit here. Sangini Bhabhi will manage on her own. *Yaar*, this is what irritates me the most. The moment the party starts, all ladies disappear into the kitchen."

Tamanna smiled and sat down, but she looked extremely uncomfortable. She kept looking towards the kitchen. It appeared as if she did not want to spend any time in the room without Sangini.

Happy looked at me questioningly. I shrugged. My mood was completely off. For me, it was a reminder of Tamanna's behaviour during our initial parties. I did not deserve this. I had eagerly waited for seven days—SEVEN LOOOOONG DAYS—to see her again. And she was behaving as if I meant nothing to her.

Perhaps, Happy understood what the matter was. "Buddy, beer for you?" he asked Sanjay.

"Yes, yes," Sanjay promptly responded.

"And, Tamanna, what will you have? Wine, breezer, or beer?"

Hesitantly, Tamanna settled for red wine. Happy got up and played the dice. "Okay, I will get beer for all of us. Meanwhile, Arjun, why don't you serve wine to Tamanna?"

"Sure," I replied without any smile on my face. I poured the wine in a glass and carefully kept it on the side table next to where Tamanna was sitting. Not even once did I look at her. It required tremendous self control, but I was really pissed off.

Happy tried more to help me. He started talking about *Love Aaj Kal* and then commented, "Man! Isn't Deepika looking awesome in it?"

This was a sensitive topic for me. In my mind, I answered, *Who needs a dummy when the real woman is sitting with us?*

"Hmmm. Well, I don't think so. I think Deepika is too dark and thin. Her features are not that good either," Sanjay replied.

Idiot, worthless man! That's why you don't value Tamanna. You have no idea what real beauty is.

"Oh come on, man! That's not true," Happy said and looked at me. "Arjun, what's your take on Deepika Padukone?" He winked.

"No comments!" I smiled and politely replied.

"Snacks for everyone!" Sangini entered the room with two big trays just then. Tamanna got up and helped her with the plates.

When everybody had been served snacks, Happy Go Lucky leaned and said to Tamanna, "Arjun is very shy while talking about his preferences. Did he ever tell you that he is absolutely crazy about Deepika?"

Instead of Tamanna, Sanjay replied, "Well, he might have told you separately. I have no idea about this fan-ship." From his tone, it was clear he was not joking but complaining that he had been treated unfairly.

"Sanjay, please, enough!" Tamanna reprimanded Sanjay, but in a casual manner.

Before anything else could be said, Happy quickly took the topic from movies to holidays, and in the next half an hour, at least half of the world was covered, mostly by Sanjay. This was one of his favourite topics, because it allowed him to show off his travel history, which contained trips to Europe, Far East, and the USA. In great detail, he told us about their lavish hotel stays, his meticulous planning of the trips, his selection of the finest places to visit, his knowledge about restaurants and alcohol from different parts of the world, and his ability to get just the best everywhere.

Sanjay's intention behind showing off all this was perhaps to make me jealous, but jealousy was an alien phenomenon for me. I was simply feeling sorry for myself and, more importantly, for my dear Sangini, that I had not been able to take her on any trips abroad.

Then, suddenly I remembered Jyoti's words, "Never begrudge your life." After that, Sanjay's speech had no effect on me.

"I love meeting new people and exploring cultures different from ours. It's a great learning experience," Sanjay concluded his speech and turned to me. "Enough about me. Arjun, man, you tell me, have you been to any country outside India?"

That didn't make me feel bad at all. "No, never got the chance."

"Dude, you don't *get* chances. You have to create them."

"I agree, but then it's not important to go out of India to meet new people and have great learning experiences. You can meet people anywhere, even in Delhi, like I did yesterday, at the Mayapuri crossing." I had no plans of bringing Jyoti into the conversation, but it appeared like the most appropriate example at that time to support my claim.

"Wh-what, who are you talking about?" Tamanna seemed really interested to know whom I had met. Sanjay smirked.

Before I could tell the whole story, Sangini took over and narrated the incident till the end wonderfully well, word to word. From her tone, it was clear that she was really proud of me. I felt like I had topped some national-level exam.

During the narration, I glanced at Tamanna a couple of times and each time I found her listening attentively and smiling gleefully. She seemed like she had come second in the exam I had topped. Happy looked intrigued, like any person would be when listening to something unusual and interesting, but Sanjay remained expressionless. He sipped his beer quietly.

After finishing the monologue, Sangini looked around, waiting for responses. Happy's was the first to come, "Wow, dude. I am proud of you!"

The baby elephant was next. He placed his hand limpidly on my arm, and trying hard to smile, said, "Good, dude. Good compassion."

Now, it was Tamanna's turn. She was smiling and laughing and shaking her head and glancing at me again and again. It seemed like she was really relieved. Finally, she spoke up, "Sangini, I have only one thing to say. You are very, very lucky."

Now I felt like I had topped a global-level exam.

For the rest of the evening, Happy kept the baby elephant engaged in conversation by talking about topics where Sanjay could show off abundantly. Meanwhile, for the first time, Tamanna talked to me in Sanjay's presence freely and openly. Of course, she addressed and looked at Sangini from time to time, but it was me she primarily talked to.

She asked more questions about Jyoti and my car ride with her and lauded my guts for driving around Delhi with a eunuch in my car. There came a time when Sangini got up to check on Sanghmitra, and Tamanna talked to me and only me for twenty minutes, looking into my eyes constantly the entire time.

Twenty minutes! This was the first time that we had maintained eye contact for so long. And I was going mad. Our close proximity and her smiling eyes took me into another world. While one part of me was answering her questions, the other part was silently unloading all its desires, questions, and complaints.

What disturbed you, Tamanna. Five calls you made. Then the whole day your phone was off. You didn't think about me even once? Oh Tamanna! I am so confused; you remain inside me, deep inside me all the time. You know, I have written poems . . . poems for you, but I can't even show them to you. Do you have any idea of what is happening with me? I have gone insane, Tamanna, I am crazy about you.

The magical and much-awaited evening got over much sooner than I would have liked—which was never.

"Both of you were terrific hosts tonight!" Tamanna said before going.

"Thanks for coming, *yaar*. I had a really nice time today after a long time," Sangini replied.

While they both embraced, Happy came to me and opened his arms. I gave him a big, tight hug. He had helped immensely in making the evening a success. It had been only because of him that I had been able to talk to Tamanna properly for the first time at my home.

As we walked outside, I remained behind Tamanna and Sangini, who were already planning the next evening. Sanjay and Happy were in the front, talking about Sanjay's trip to Spain. I walked with my cell phone tightly gripped in my hand.

It contained the purest feelings for the one who was walking in front of me—my secret verses for Tamanna.

'Is this real, God? Are these poems really for her?' I continuously wondered within my heart.

18

The next morning, the first thing I did was checking the Notes app on my phone. I had composed another verse, at 3.52 a.m. When I jogged my memory, I vaguely remembered getting up and looking for my phone.

This new verse had a story in it, of how bad I felt when Tamanna had behaved distantly and coldly in the beginning last evening, and how everything changed when I brought Jyoti into the conversation. The intensity of the verse was mesmerising, at least for me. I slowly started humming my dad's favourite song.

Imagine me and you, I do,
I think about you day and night.

After having a lovely breakfast with my family, I typed an SMS for Happy: *Thanks bro! You handled things so well. Your presence made all the difference.*

He replied in a minute: *OH…don't embarrass me…that was my duty yaar. What are friends for man? But you are a lucky guy. Sangini is truly an angel, and so is Tamanna. I think both are of same height…didn't notice last time. Both look terrific in their own way…lucky guy!*

"Bastard," I smiled and closed the message box.

Was I a "lucky guy"? Or was I entering into a spider's web?

In the afternoon, Sanghmitra expressed a desire to watch the *Lord of the Rings* trilogy. Her wish was my command. So I went out and bought the DVDs. While watching them, my phone rang. I was in no mood to attend any calls on a Sunday afternoon and would have ignored it had Sangini not passed on the phone to me. "It is Sanjay," she said. She was visibly surprised and so was I.

"Hi dude," Sanjay greeted me unenthusiastically.

"Hi, man . . . Good to hear from you," I replied politely.

"I wanted to thank you for the dinner yesterday."

"Oh, no problem. It was our pleasure."

"Yes, yes," he said and came to the real reason behind the call. "By the way, man, that Jyoti story was really heart touching. Umm, I hope everything was real and you didn't really do anything." He laughed.

My temper rose. I was on the verge of saying something rude when I recalled Happy's advice. *You got to play your cards smartly. You must give Sanjay importance. Don't piss him off.* So I calmed myself down and gently asked, "What do you mean by 'do anything'?"

Suddenly, baby elephant's tone became friendly, "Ooh Arjun, you are a very serious guy. You take everything too seriously."

This man worshipped his gods, whom he had never met, but could never respect other human beings. People like Jyoti have to feel inferior from the likes of him, even though they may be a hundred times better person. "I'm sorry. That . . . maybe because I—"

"Actually, on Friday, Tamanna and I were passing through the Mayapuri crossing and I saw you talking to that eunuch. I have seen her quite a number of times around that place. Then I saw her entering your car . . ."

Suddenly everything fell into place in my mind. *That is why Tamanna called five times. That is why she behaved weirdly initially yesterday. She thought I and Jyoti—oh my God!*

Sanjay was saying some nasty things about Jyoti's appearance and sexuality. I kept quiet. I wanted to end the conversation as quickly as possible.

"Hey, I will soon come to your office to take some guidance for my school's website," he said at the end.

I welcomed him to come anytime and we said our goodbyes.

"What happened?" Sangini asked.

"Nothing. He wants to come to the office for some help regarding his school's website," I answered and we resumed watching the movie.

However, I was no longer interested in Frodo and Gandalf's exploits. My mind was abuzz with what must have happened on Friday. On seeing me with Jyoti, Sanjay must have assumed that I was picking her up to hook up with and he must've then shared this with Tamanna, who must have gotten extremely disturbed and had ended up calling me again and again. On finding my phone out of network area, her suspicions must have deepened. That explained why she was so relieved to learn about Jyoti from Sangini yesterday. Her missed calls showed how concerned she was about me.

I have a place in her heart.

Now, I wanted to desperately call her up and confirm everything. But there was no question of making that call on a Sunday, when I was with my family and she was probably with hers. So I fervently waited for the next day.

That night, I met Tamanna in her own house in my dreams. Both of us were talking freely, while Sanjay roamed around the house smoking and talking on phone. He never came to disturb us. Such a lovely dream it was!

I woke up to find another poem in my Notes app. This one was about waiting for a complete day to talk to Tamanna.

It was a breezy August morning. I dressed up, said bye to Sanghmitra, who was going for a school picnic, and left home after a sumptuous breakfast. I had barely moved out of my block when the screen of my cell phone became a sight of the heavens for me.

Tamanna calling.

My hands trembled as I took her call.

"Hi Arjun, how are you?" she spoke.

"Hi, Tamanna, I am fine. How are you?" I tried my best to sound normal and partially succeeded.

"I am good," she said. "It was fantastic that day."

"Yeah, it was. Thank you for coming." Then I gathered courage and casually asked, "Hey, I got f-f-five missed calls from you on Friday. My phone was probably out of range at that time. I forgot to ask you about it on Saturday. Was it something urgent? I mean . . . what was . . . the matter?"

"Hmm . . . well . . ." she hesitated, "wanted to talk to you, that's it."

I wished it was true but from her tone it was clear she was lying.

So I said, "Are you sure that was the only reason? I learnt through Sanjay that both of you saw me at the Mayapuri crossing that day. Was that the reason you called me?" As soon as I said this, I regretted it. I should have restrained myself. Mentioning something that Sanjay had told me to Tamanna could be troublesome. It was unethical too—almost like bitching with a friend about her husband. It was irresponsible of me. A silly mistake.

Tamanna sighed and replied in a composed tone, "Arjun, I do not wish to take that incident any further. It makes no sense to talk about it. After learning about it, Sanjay shouldn't have brought it up . . . It was wrong on his part." She paused. "I believe whatever we do, it is our business. Nobody has any right to raise a finger at it, or try enquiring about it . . . unless the person's actions directly affect us or unless we are related closely to them."

"Tamanna, I didn't—"

"Arjun, there's just one thing," she interrupted. "I will say it but on one condition."

"Tell me please," I hastily replied. My heartbeat quickened.

"Promise me you won't ask any questions."

"Anything you say, Tamanna."

"Arjun, I am sorry I presumed something. Please forgive me."

"I-I . . . what do . . . I . . ." I was overwhelmed and speechless.

"No, nothing, you promised."

I miserably searched for words. I was breathing deeply. I couldn't believe Tamanna was speaking to me with so much emotion. It seemed she really had some feelings for me. It was like a dream come true.

"Arjun, are you there?"

"Hmm, umm, yes, yes, I am here," I managed somehow.

"Are you okay?"

"Oh yeah . . . yeah."

Go on, Tamanna, go on, don't bother about me, you speak, you just talk, I want to listen to you.

"Uhh, Arjun, I forgot, you must be driving to your office. Are you still driving or have you parked the car?"

How come she knew I was driving? Can she see me from somewhere?

"Uh, oh, well, I was driving but I stopped the car the moment your call came. How come you knew about the driving thing?"

"I have sources." She laughed. "Okay, tell me, have you made any progress with your second book?"

"No, I have been very busy," I said. *Busy composing poems for you*, I added silently.

She advised me to take some time out daily and concentrate on my book. I asked whether I could mail her the rough draft of the story.

"Sure! I will be honoured to read it. I will be waiting for your mail."

There was nothing more to be said and soon we said our goodbyes, even though I wished I could have spoken to her for at least a couple of hours more. The call had lasted about fifteen minutes. In that short duration, I felt that my relationship with Tamanna had taken a giant leap forward. Now, I knew she cared for me and her trust in me had also deepened.

When I mailed the rough draft to Tamanna the next day, Babbu loudly objected, pounding on his desk.

"You are putting your foot forward in an absolutely wrong way. There are better ways to have an affair."

"What are you talking about? Yes, I love her, but I am not having any affair with her. I am only mailing this to her because I know that she will be the best guide."

"OHH COME ON, Arjun, please stop this nasty habit of covering up your desires with philosophy."

"What is so wrong?"

"This . . . this mailing thing is risky, man! Why are you doing this when things are so much better? She's with you, you meet, talk, go on a date, and have romantic conversations. Now is the time to jiggy-jiggy. Why are you unnecessarily trying to push your book between your happiness and Tamanna? Besides, Sanjay may have her password. What if he comes to know?"

"Let him check the mail. What wrong am I doing?"

"What are you doing? Can't you see it?" Babbu looked at me in disbelief. "That narrow-minded useless bugger would never be able to digest this kind of friendship between you and Tamanna, where you two are in regular touch and she is advising you about your book. No husband would share his wife with somebody in this way." Just then, his phone rang and his eyes lit up. Clearly, it was Simmi's phone. He went out to talk to her.

Meanwhile, I sent my first message to Tamanna on its way. Babbu's advice was valid, but I was too lost in love to bother about trivialities. Whatever was to happen would happen, I thought, and I couldn't wait to see what it would be. My emotions were now unstoppable.

As the next couple of hours passed by one by one, I grew increasingly restless.

What's taking her so long?

She ought to call me now. The draft was not that long.

I must call her up now. Yes, I can do that. I now have the right to do that. I have a solid reason to do that.

"Hellewww," her joyful voice greeted me when I dialled her number.

"Hello," I chuckled. "Did you get the time to read the draft?"

"Sir, have some patience, sir. I am still not through with it." The joy in her voice was palpable. It was wonderful to hear her talk like that, to hear her call me "sir." Suddenly, my earlier impatience appeared childish to me. So, I completed the call quickly and asked her to call back whenever she was through with the reading. She responded with, "Yes, sir!"

You have no idea how dearly I have been waiting to have you like this in my life, Tamanna. You have no idea what each call, each word of yours means to me.

In the next half-hour, I copied some more photographs of Tamanna from Sanjay's Facebook folder to my computer. Although, she wasn't properly visible in any of those, at least she was in them. I wanted to have as many photographs of her as I could.

As I sat looking at the pictures, I had an idea. I called our web designer and asked him to install Photo Shop on my laptop. I had never worked with the software myself, but I had sat with our designer while he worked on it many times, so I had some idea of its functions. Over the next couple of hours, using web tutorials and through trial-and-error, I edited all the photos by carefully removing all the unwanted faces and highlighting Tamanna's face. Then I created a collage out of all the photographs and stared at it for some time, pleased with my work.

I was on my way back home when Tamanna called again. I had not been expecting her call at that hour because usually, by that time, Sanjay was at home.

I pressed accept and Tamanna immediately started talking about my story. She really liked the first draft, she said. She found it really funny. She just laughed and discussed her point of view. "It's amazing, but still needs a lot of hard work so as to become a best-seller," she concluded. "Work hard on it, sir. I will pray for your success. Let me know if you need any more help."

Each word spoken by her in the conversation meant life to me. Not even once did I ask about Sanjay or whether he was around or not. She didn't mention him either. Obviously, she was calling me in his absence. I took that for granted.

On a whim, I told Sangini everything about my call and the mail to Tamanna. She was surprised to hear about this sudden surge in our friendship, but in the end, she said, "She is a smart girl. You will certainly benefit from her advice." That's all she said. But I was probably expecting something more from her . . .

That confused me. She seemed to be withholding her feelings. She had used very limited words for her response. Alarm bells started ringing in my head. On thinking about it later, I realized that she had not said anything about Sanjay or what he might think about this sudden development. Her crisp and controlled response bothered me! I was expecting her to say more about Sanjay's bitching, to comment on Tamanna's concern regarding my book, and call up Tamanna and discuss the whole issue just like good friends. They were good friends after all! But that didn't happen. A web of confusion started building in my mind regarding my sharing of the whole episode with Sangini.

In my opinion I had played very carelessly. 'Silly' would be the right word to describe my action. Just like the previous occasion, I could have hidden this conversation also, but I didn't. Love, sometimes, results in strange fears and actions. Mine was one such case.

19

There were no conversations between me and Tamanna through the rest of the week. She didn't call, and neither did I. Although I constantly longed to hear her voice, that week wasn't so bad because I had the assurance that my love for her was not for naught. She really cared about me and maybe even had feelings for me.

It felt like a very intoxicating and fantastic period had started in my life. I smiled for no reason. I sang for no reason. I frequently joked in our business meetings with our clients, and surprisingly, would hear jokes from them too. It was as if my love had influenced everyone. Many times, I would involuntarily type whatever I was feeling for her on my mobile and save it in the Notes app. My love verses also continued alongside. In that week, I had created three new verses in the middle of the night.

The next Monday, at 9.15 a.m., I received a text from Babbu: *Going to paint the town red today.....Will be meeting Simmi in South-Ex at 10:15 am. Your friend is finally settled. Bye lover boy!*

That made me smile. Babbu's story had progressed rather quickly. That prodded me to take a step forward myself. I parked my car in the parking lot near the office and my fingers rushed for Tamanna's name in my contact list. Crossing my fingers and hoping for Sanjay's absence, I dialled the number.

"Helleowsss," Tamanna's joyful voice greeted me. She was really happy to get my call!

That made me bold. "I have been thinking of talking to you the whole week," I said confidently.

"So was I," Tamanna replied without any hesitation.

Wow! Wow! Wow! Would she ever come to know that she is the goddess of happiness for me?

"Really?" I laughed in joy.

"Yessss, sir!" the goddess continued to mesmerise me. "But I couldn't call. The whole week we were busy with the sudden arrival of Sanjay's brother and his family from Finland. I hardly had time to rest."

I was immensely relieved to learn that. Tamanna had a valid reason of not calling me up!

"So, did you move any further with the story?" she asked.

I was drowning in so much happiness that I couldn't think of a response.

"Hellooooo?" she checked.

"Hmmm, yeah," I responded. "No, I didn't . . ." I felt ashamed.

"Arjun, you would never be able to complete the book like this," she sounded concerned. "Don't waste too much of time thinking. Thinking must be followed by action."

She said some more encouraging words before disconnecting the. It was a short call but it made my day. It also made me decide to work on my book. I didn't want to disappoint Tamanna the next time we talked.

That afternoon, I quickly finished my lunch and opened the word file of the rough draft of my story on my computer.

I glued myself to the screen, penetrating deep into each line I had written, but somehow, I felt stuck.

Was it because of the gap of so many years between the creation and the present times? Or maybe my own mental frame had changed and my level of maturity had moved forward a great deal? Or maybe the unseen destiny and the all powerful universe had some other design for me?

After a long period of struggle, Sangini and I had been able to change a lot within ourselves, and thus, a lot had changed for the better in our relationship too. And also, Tamanna was there in my life. My soul was getting nourished and my inner happiness was touching new heights.

I was getting the most treasured gift of human life. Financial struggles were temporary. I think that I had learnt a great deal about how to lead this treasured human life. I had learnt how to correctly understand its ups and downs. I had learnt to persevere in life and fight back, and fight for victory. So, in totality, the weather in the inside world of my mortal body was fantastic.

Our professional vehicle too had gained considerable momentum, though financial gains were still elusive. But I was not worried. We were on the right track.

Whenever I would sit and think about moving forward with my story, my mind would resound with some strange echoing whispers—*The truth of your heart . . . your heart . . . love . . . sacred love . . . pure love . . . Tamanna . . . Sangini . . .* '

No matter how sincerely I would try to work on my story, I would always and absolutely involuntarily end up typing my feelings on the notepad of my cell phone. And my sleeping nights would witness the creation of love verses in the same dazed state.

That weekend, I tried inviting Sanjay and Tamanna for

dinner, but it got cancelled. Sanjay's brother had extended his stay in India. Tamanna herself called up Sangini to inform her. Sangini said it seemed that Tamanna really wanted to come and was very apologetic about not being able to make it.

So another week passed before I heard again from Tamanna. On Tuesday, I was sitting in the office and reading the verse I had created the previous night. My soul was embedded deep into its every word. My breathing was slow and deep. I was pining for her.

Ohhhh Tamanna!

Just then my phone beeped. Quite listlessly, I picked it up. When I looked at the screen, I was filled with joy. It was an SMS from Tamanna.

Ohh, thanks, thanks so much, God! Thanks Tamanna! Thanks so much!

Without wasting a heartbeat, I opened the message. It said: *So, Mr. Writer any progress so far?*

Ohhhhh God! She cares for me. She has been thinking about me.

Instead of texting, I immediately pressed the 'Call' button.

"Helleowssss," Tamanna's usual joyous tone greeted me.

Tears of happiness filled my eyes. My feelings were on the tip of my tongue, but I controlled myself.

"How are you, Tamanna?" I asked in a voice heavy with emotions.

She took a moment to answer. "I am fine. But you sound overwrought and a bit tired too. What's wrong?"

Gosh! How did she guess that? She sees right through me!

"Hey Mr. Writerrrr? What's up?" she asked.

"Uhh, nothing much. Your SMS was a coincidence. I was thinking about you only." I blurted without thinking much. All thought seemed a waste of time.

Again, she took a moment to reply. I waited with bated breath.

"Really?" She laughed. "That's an honour, sir. I thought you had forgotten me. No communication in the last seven days . . ."

That made me laugh with boundless happiness.

"I thought you would call and update me about your progress with the book," she continued. "But, I think sir was very busy!" Now she was teasing me.

I tried responding but my reaction was devoid of any intelligent words. "I . . ." I laughed. "I . . ." I laughed more, struggling with my reply.

She too laughed. "What? You what?"

"No, nothing! That is not true, I mean . . . I wasn't that busy. I mean . . . I . . ." I laughed some more.

"I know Arjun, I was just kidding. I too never called you in the last week. We all get busy."

"Hmm," I hmm-ed. "Anyway, I am really confused, Tamanna. I don't know how to progress with the story."

"Confusion is part of human life. When confused, you must intensify your prayers and efforts. Please don't remain for too long in this state," she advised.

I had a feeling that she was not convinced with my reply, but didn't say anything. She concluded the call by asking me to take it easy. I, on the other hand, tried coming up with a worthy topic for conversation, but failed.

After disconnecting, I opened the collage with Tamanna's photos and stared at it for some time, smiling. Babbu returned from a meeting and brought me back to work. As usual, he was all smiles. His last week's date with Simmi had been a thunderous success. It was incredible how well they had connected after fifteen long years of staying out of touch. He was now desperately searching for a room. They needed some privacy to "discuss important things" after all.

Meanwhile, I had stopped sharing updates about Tamanna with him. There was no point telling him anything. Our worlds were too different. If I felt like talking to someone, I preferred to call up or visit Happy.

Later that day, while having tea, I opened the Tamanna collage again. At about 5.50 p.m., my phone rang. It was one of our vendors. I went to the washroom while talking to the man, leaving behind the open computer screen with Tamanna everywhere on it.

While concluding the call inside the washroom, I heard some voices. I could hear Babbu greeting someone in the visitor's area. I tried to concentrate. The visitor's voice was familiar but I couldn't place it. Due to the noise coming from outside the washroom window, it was difficult to identify who was speaking. I quickly washed my hands and pressed my ear to the door. Then I got a jolt.

Sanjay! Fuck!

"Arjun is just coming. This is our small office," Babbu was saying.

MY LAPTOP! MY LAPTOP!

I had kept it at such an angle that Babbu could not see it from his seat. But in the process, I had placed it in such a way that anyone entering the cabin could easily see it.

With my heart hammering in my chest, I frantically searched for a way out to prevent Sanjay from laying an eye on my screen. I thought of calling up Babbu on his phone. But I realized that might prove to be suicidal, for if Babbu's phone was in the cabin, he would rush inside to take the call, and Sanjay would simply follow him and see photographs of his wife stolen from his Facebook account on my computer screen.

My situation was unimaginable. I had never thought, not even in my wildest of daydreams, that the truth of my love would be revealed in this way. My shirt was almost wet with sweat.

I considered calling up Tamanna and apologising from the bottom of my heart for everything. I would take the blame on myself. It was my love after all, not hers. I knew the repercussions. My family life would be shattered again. And Sangini? What will she think about all this? What will she do?

"OHH MY GOD!" I almost cried.

I could now make out that they had moved inside the cabin. My heart sank completely. Just then, my phone beeped.

Asshole lover boy…..I saved your life today! No danger …everything okay. Now come out and dance with your girlfriend's husband.

I read the SMS in disbelief and then closed my eyes and heaved an exceptionally long sigh of relief. I was so relieved, SOOO relieved to read that. A feeling of gratitude overflowed from my heart in leaps and bounds for Babbu.

I came out and turned towards the cabin. Both the guys were talking merrily. My laptop screen was blank.

As I entered the cabin, Babbu said, "See, our sir has come out."

Sanjay turned his head towards me. "So dude, see how I have finally blessed your office with my presence." He was sitting on the same chair where I had been sitting a while back and admiring his wife's photographs. This thought pricked my heart like a needle.

I exchanged pleasantries with him and took the visitor's chair. Ten minutes passed. Babbu was being extra nice to Sanjay. He had ordered samosas, pastries, and coffee.

My phone beeped again with Babbu's SMS. *Your girlfriend's husband after all………must get full attention from us!*

I read it but didn't react. Though I conversed normally, a feeling of extreme discomfort had engulfed me. For me, even looking at Sanjay had become difficult. I was feeling shattered.

Today the game was almost finished. This man sitting in front of you is Tamanna's husband. She is his wife, his life partner, his better half. She's the mother of his child! Have you been sleeping, Arjun? Wake up! Tamanna is married to this man sitting in front of you. She cooks food for him, takes care of him, sleeps with him. She is his, and he is hers. WAKE UP, ARJUN!

"Hey dude! Are you ok?" Sanjay asked. All my discomfort had probably made it to my face.

"No . . . nothing. Just tired after a long day."

Does he know about our telephone conversations?

Sanjay was there because he had work for us. He and his big-shot brother from Finland were starting an advertising agency.

"I have personal contacts in Reliance, Tata, Larsen and Tourbo, MGF, DLF, Bausch & Laumb." He casually threw around names as we took him through our presentation.

"That's great, man." Babbu said appreciatively. "You would have no problem in getting customers."

The big-shot nodded. "I know." He looked at both of us, as if saying, *"See, this is how big I am!"* Then he announced, "In the first year, I have a small target of generating business worth 10 crore."

I was least interested in all this crap. But Babbu looked impressed.

"See, we are starting on a big platform," he continued. "And I want my friends to benefit from it too." He looked at me while saying this. "I had to outsource all this work, so I thought, why not give it to my own friends? You must also grow and benefit from me."

His arrogance was now irritating the hell out of me. He sounded as if he was giving us alms.

Our table was now full of snacks and coffee. Sanjay kept talking, and I kept failing to make sense of his claims. They had no office, no team, and no setup yet. He said he would be hiring people from top MNCs and offering them stakes in his company. He had identified an office space in Gurgaon, for which he had an ambiguous story. In the end, he promised all audio-visual and creative work to us.

"You people are already doing it on a small scale. Now stretch your arms! Arjun, now even you will get a chance to grow really big in life!"

I smiled. I was trying my best to control my temper. But Babbu seemed to have gotten convinced. "So, how should we proceed?" he asked.

"Hmmm, let's make a website first of all. Tomorrow I will send my man. He is assisting me in the project," Sanjay replied. Then casually he added, "See, in the beginning I am on a shoestring budget. But you know where we are finally heading, right?"

Babbu nodded gleefully. But I was not at all convinced. I was feeling very uncomfortable. A creepy, hollow feeling clouded my mind. According to me, Sanjay's claims completely lacked logic and wisdom.

This man is just not capable of benefitting anyone.

Then I wondered whether Tamanna was the reason behind my discomfort. Maybe Sanjay was talking sense, but because of my bias and my love, I was so reluctant to believe and trust him that I doubted everything he was saying.

The meeting took rather long, about one and a half hours. Twice Sanjay's phone rang in that period. He was sitting next to me, and I could see his phone. Both times, its screen said,

"Wife Calling." He picked the call up on both occasions, but hurriedly disconnected after saying he was in a general meeting. It was strange. He never mentioned my name.

When the meeting ended, we proceeded to the exit. Sanjay never said anything about my phone calls to Tamanna.

He still doesn't know anything about our new friendship? I wondered and worried.

"So? Any news of your Jyoti?" Sanjay questioned me as he was about to leave.

"What?" I asked.

"OHH, my saint friend! She's attractive! I think she can be a good experiment, a real nice one."

I just smiled and shook my head in negative. My words would have been a complete wastage on a man like him. Normally, I would have discussed the possibility of our dinner get-togethers. But that day I found myself uncomfortable doing that.

20

Later that night, while having dinner with Sangini, I told her everything about the meeting with Sanjay. Like me, she too felt that something was fishy, that Sanjay was building castles in the air.

"Let him do what he wants with his advertising project," she advised. "But, please, for the website and all, ask for the money in advance. We need money, Arjun . . . you know that very well." She paused. "Work and friendship are two different things. Don't ever mix them. I am not asking you to take unreasonable amounts of money, but at least take money for the resources that you will be putting in."

I nodded silently.

"Don't misunderstand me, please! I never want to interfere in your work. But you are no longer in a position to render favours to people, honey, least of all to people who are, by God's grace, already well placed in life. You have done that enough in your life. You have painstakingly devoted most of your life to people. Now it is the time for your family. Promise me that you will do the right thing."

"Yes, I will."

I didn't mind anything that Sangini said. She was speaking from experience. For years, she had witnessed the shameless thanklessness of most people for whom I had always selflessly opened the doors of my heart and home. She had seen me being betrayed by people I considered a vital part of my support system.

***

It was 11.21 p.m. Both my dolls had slept. Finally, I had time to be with myself, to clearly hear the sound of my heart and try to understand the significance of my day's acts. While thinking about Sanjay's sudden entry in the office, I was still getting jitters. I lay down on the bed with the lights switched off and tried to establish a connection with my higher self.

Aren't you on a wrong track?

Please, stop here, Arjun!

Please, God, help me forget Tamanna.

My whole body shook frighteningly.

Tamanna is deep inside my heart . . .

I felt as if my body was a deep ocean. I tightly closed my eyes. I felt as if the whole universe had become encompassed in my five-feet-ten-inch frame and was reverberating with the sound of my consciousness.

I love Tamanna. But she is not mine. Only my love is mine.

I love Tamanna. I don't want her physical possession. Why would I want it anyway? She's already there inside me.

My love can never make her unhappy. I will see to it that she is always happy in her family life. She is Sanjay's wife. Only my love is mine. She will never come to know about my love.

I was in a mystical state of deep meditation.

Tamanna is inside me. Then where is Sangini?

And if I had boundless love for Sangini, how could I ever justify my actions towards Tamanna?

I felt as if I was floating in the vast universe.

Where is Sangini?

I could clearly visualise her glowing face as if I was watching her on a big screen. I smiled.

Sangini is my wife, my love. She is everywhere inside me and will remain there forever.

I was slipping deep into slumber. I could feel the absolute calmness of the universe. That night I had an unusually relaxing sleep, deep and dreamless.

***

The next day, I felt none of the emotions of the previous day—no anger, no uneasiness, no guilt. Instead, I was experiencing a strange conviction. My life could not move on and on like this. Tamanna would not go anywhere from my life, I'd realised that. But, then, I could not have any expectations from her, I could not move any further with her. That would be like playing with fire. That would be stupid and immoral.

After a long time, I was thinking rationally.

I vowed to keep the world of love for Tamanna in my heart safely, and pray for my wisdom, so that I could maintain a normal relationship with her and Sanjay. I had no idea yet of what my approach was going to be, but there was a strong conviction in my heart and I knew I'd figure a way out.

***

The next twenty days saw hectic activity in our office due to Sanjay's work. Every day, his associate would turn up at 10.00 a.m. sharp and would stay the whole day. Soon, we realised that the scope of Sanjay's work was far beyond our assumptions. His aspirations, his demands were sky-high. His website needed advanced technology. Some of its aspects were beyond our expertise and required a lot of research. Our entire team worked painstakingly, so much so that our routine work for our existing schools—our major source of bread and butter—started getting delayed. Our office hours stretched from nine to twelve hours.

Needless to say, we also began using a sizable amount of resources for Sanjay's work and our costs of operation—including the staff's remuneration for working overtime and essentials like electricity, tea, coffee, etc.—escalated each day. It did not take us long to conclude that not talking clearly about the financial implications of the work with Sanjay beforehand was a big blunder on our part.

These hectic days were even more difficult for me because while on one hand I was consistent in my prayers, trying my best to deepen my conviction to not obsess about Tamanna, on the other hand, I kept composing love verses for her in the middle of the night. My laptop folder containing these strange creations of my heart kept increasing steadily with each passing week. As if that was not enough, I had to regularly sit and chat with the man whose wife was a portion of my soul.

As more and more time passed, the amount of effort required to keep Tamanna out of my mind increased. My heart and mind were constantly at war with each other. Repressing my love was like trying to push back a lofty Himalayan peak into the earth. I felt like I was trying to ignore my reflection in the mirror while looking right into it.

I learnt that certain things are easier said than done. Convictions are easy to be declared in a fit of rage or at a low point in life, but after a while, dormant desires become active again and begin playing with our minds. They deceive us and try to surface in various forms and emotions. Unless your defences are rock solid, the river of desires overflows sooner or later . . . like it happened one day with me when, unable to control myself, I went out of the office and called up Tamanna.

As the bell started ringing, I began to curse myself for being weak. But I could not disconnect the phone now. I felt the hotness rushing into my veins.

"Hi Arjun! You have a long life."

She was thinking about me only!

"Hi Tamanna," I quickly composed myself and responded.

"Hmmm. Tell me, what's the matter?" Her voice was sweet and comforting. "Something is bothering Arjun. Arjun seems to be deeply worried. What could it be?"

No, Tamanna, no! Don't be so intuitive. I will weaken. No . . . please! I shouldn't have called you at all.

Completely unaware of my condition, Tamanna continued, "Can Tamanna help Arjun in any way? Tamanna is really good at counselling her friends."

The truth was on the tip of my tongue. I had to fight with myself to search for a lie. I found it in my inability to move further with my book.

Tamanna heard me very patiently and responded in an extremely affectionate tone, "You know, Arjun, sometimes our destiny, which is of course framed by our karma, wants to pull us back from our current direction and lead us towards some unknown direction. Maybe that's what is happening with you. Don't get confused or agitated. Just trust your prayers."

To me it seemed as if she had kissed the forehead of my soul with that reply.

Oh Tamanna, you beautiful, beautiful woman. Do you have any idea how much your Arjun has missed you?

I thanked her for her reply and she asked me about Sangini. Then the topic came to their house and Sanjay's Finland-returned brother.

"Together both the brothers are planning some new venture. Our house is always abuzz with the sound of children. I really like that."

"Of course, I know about all that. Sanjay's associate visits my office every day to work on the project," I said.

She took a while before replying. "Is it?" She was clearly surprised, as if it was news to her. Alarm bells started ringing in my head. "He is so busy these days; always very tied up . . . perhaps he missed out on this one."

Suddenly but affectionately, she terminated the call as the kids were making too much of noise. But before she disconnected, she said, "Arjun, take it easy and have faith in the higher power."

***

"Oh come on, dude, what's so difficult about this? Every other website company can do this. Show me how good you are," Sanjay said on phone and laughed.

When we disconnected, I told Babbu we should ask the baby elephant for advance money in the meeting later that evening.

Babbu was unconcerned. "I was thinking that too," he said. "But, you know, for me, a girlfriend's husband is as important as my wife's brother."

I burst out laughing.

"I know how difficult it is for you to tell me this," my friend continued. "To ask for money from her husband. I know, man, I know you are doing this for me, so that I do not feel bad thinking we are doing a free project in the name of your love."

"Shut the fuck up!" I laughed again.

He leaned back in his chair and sighed. "Erm, okay, I will ask for money today. But you remain out of this."

Gosh! Babbu was taking it all wrong. But it was a blessing in disguise—now I won't have to go through the discomfort of asking Sanjay for money. So I kept mum.

That evening, Babbu tried explaining to Sanjay the magnitude and the scale of the work and the basic resources needed for his project. The baby elephant nodded and responded with a few *"I know, I know"* and *"I understand dude."*

"So much is happening right now and I am under so much stress. I have only nine thousand in my wallet right. You take seven out of it as your pocket money." With that he took out seven thousand rupees from his wallet and showed us the remaining two thousand.

I didn't like his tone and attitude, but I was glad he had shelled out some money. Just then, his phone rang. Eagerly, I looked at his mobile screen. "Wife calling," the screen said. He quickly picked the phone from the table and went out of the cabin. That hurt me. It had been almost a week since I'd heard Tamanna's voice. I tried to control my feelings and strengthen my conviction.

"Well, well, he has surprised me," Babbu said as he counted the currency notes.

I took out my phone and started typing in my Notes app mechanically. I wanted to vent out the pain of seeing her name on the screen of Sanjay's phone and my inability to call her up and talk to her.

"What happened, man? What are you typing so fast?"

I could reply only with, "Hmmm." My heart and soul were in the stream of text that was appearing on my mobile screen almost magically. With each typed word, the craving for Tamanna increased exponentially in my heart. After a few moments, Sanjay returned. Reflexively, I closed the Notes window and kept my phone back on the table. But too late.

"Dude, you can complete that message. Not a problem," Sanjay commented as he sat down.

I was too overwrought with emotions to become normal again quickly. I just smiled in response.

"What? Did I say something very unusual, dude?"

"Nothing . . . ehh . . . absolutely!" I fumbled. "I wasn't typing anything significant. Excuse me."

I got up and went out. I urgently needed to lighten up my mind. Otherwise, I might have said something stupid to Sanjay.

***

Over the next few days, Sanjay asked Babbu to book eight new domains for two new projects he was planning with his brother. Our costs escalated.

On day twenty of Sanjay's project, Babbu and I were discussing the investment we had made so far on it. The numbers were too large and we were worried.

Just then my phone beeped. It was an SMS from Sangini: *Send ur peon home. I hv a surprise fr u."*

I was startled. Sangini had never done such a thing before. My nerve cells started tingling. I showed the message to Babbu.

Babbu was surprised too. "Has she come to know about Tamanna and all?"

That was the most idiotic thing I had ever heard. "Tamanna?" I almost shouted at him. "And she will call our office peon to discuss it? Is it?"

I replied to the text: *Wat? Anything special?*

Sangini typed back: *No further communication plz. Send ur peon.*

I had no choice but to instruct our peon to do the needful. But before he left, I ordered him to call me as soon as he left my home and tell us about whatever surprise Sangini had to give him.

About fifty minutes passed.

"God, save my friend today," Babbu murmured.

The all-important call came. I immediately disconnected the call and called back.

"Yes?" I asked curiously.

"Sir, madam has given a tiffin box."

"That's it? Nothing else?"

The reply was in negative. I disconnected the call and laughed as I guessed what the whole deal was about. In the initial years of our marriage, Sangini used to surprise me a lot with "surprise dishes." She would prepare something nice after learning painstakingly from the recipe books, but won't declare anything to me. At dinner, she would suddenly bring it and keep it in front of me.

When our peon arrived, Babbu hastily opened the box and asked him to get two spoons. It was a sweet dish. With a garnishing of freshly cut fruits like strawberries, kiwis, apples, bananas and a layer of cake crumbs on the top, it seemed like a well-prepared fruit pudding.

Wasting no time, I called up Sangini.

"Yesssss please?" Sangini's joyful tone greeted me.

"What should I say? I am speechless."

"No, no, remaining speechless won't help today," she replied, sounding really happy. "Your appreciation is necessary here. Else it would be an injustice to someone's great efforts. So please be ready with your appreciation, Arjun Sir."

Someone's great efforts?

The next voice on the phone was not of Sangini's.

"Hello, Arjun Sir."

In a flash of a second, I made sense of everything. My heart pounded with excitement.

"Hi, Tamanna . . ."

"I hope you liked my ordinary dish."

"NOOO! It isn't ordinary," I could hear Sangini shouting, "it is the most delicious sweet dish I have ever tasted."

I laughed.

"She is too generous," Tamanna said. "Actually that day I couldn't prepare the caramel custard. So today, I thought of compensating for that time and prepare a better dish. And since both of you have got a sweet tooth, I couldn't wait to bring it freshly prepared for you guys."

My happiness was simply unexplainable. I knew that the dish had been prepared especially for me. I grabbed the lunch box from Babbu and did not let him have another spoon. Spoon by spoon, as the custard went inside me, something transformed there. From that moment onwards, Tamanna's physical proximity stopped mattering to me. I stopped caring when I would be talking to her next, when I would be seeing her face next, how easygoing she would be with me, for how many seconds we would talk for.

I felt like I was always in her mind. The custard filled a vacuum that had been inside me for three years.

***

Same day after dinner, Sangini brought few spoons of the dish in a saucer. "Here, we will have it together in this," she said. "Arjun, there is something that really touched me today. What Tamanna did today for us, I had done the same with so many in the past. But they all turned thankless. More than me, I feel bad for you. You have done marvelous things for people. But what you got in return was highly painful. But today when Tamanna asked me if I could send some portion of the dish to you in your office as a surprise, I really liked that. I liked that because she did it for you. It has been ages since I saw someone doing something so wonderful for you."

I had no words. Only Sangini was capable of such positive thinking.

"In my life till date, I haven't seen such opposite poles," Sangini continued. "Sanjay's presence makes me uncomfortable, while Tamanna is an angel. She gives such comforting vibes. I feel nice to see that you are attracting well-meaning friendships. It doesn't matter even if they are from the most unlikely quarters. But better be careful about Sanjay's project."

Saying this, she got up from her chair and went inside the kitchen.

21

The flavour of Tamanna's awesome sweet dish lingered in my mouth for many days. My mind, meanwhile, continued to create verse after verse for her in an even more feverish state. At the same time, I tried to normalise my relationship with Sanjay, who, on many occasions, would enter our office when I would be looking at photographs of his wife on my laptop.

One day, he came in looking very disturbed. I instantly got worried.

Has he learnt about Tamanna and me? This was the first thought that came to my mind.

But, thank God, it was something else. "My brother . . ." Sanjay explained with a deep sigh. "He has suffered a huge loss in his business back in Finland."

"Uhh oh!" I exclaimed.

Sanjay continued, "Two million dollars . . . One of his employees backstabbed him! He siphoned off the money and is now absconding." He told us the whole story in detail. By the end of it, his eyes were moist. He had an unshaven beard of three-four days and looked completely distraught. According to him, it was a major setback for the family. Their whole business plan was now jeopardised. Everyone was in a state of shock.

The whole incident touched me deeply. Because of

my financial history, I could feel his pain acutely. I could totally empathise with his situation and wanted to hug him and comfort him with soothing words. In one second, I pardoned him for all his past mistakes. I couldn't give him a hug, but I squeezed his arm reassuringly many times. I told him everything would be all right, and that he should pray to God for the best. I also prayed for him within my heart. He spent nearly three hours in our office that day. Babbu and I tried to change his mood and cracked jokes often.

At the end, very politely, he asked about the website progress. After such a shocker, his brother was depending on this new venture for financial support.

"Don't worry, brother, we will complete it in the next few days," I responded.

Sanjay tried to smile. "Uhh, I know the project's scale has escalated. I will try to arrange your payments. It will be—"

"Don't be stupid," I shouted him down. "You pay when you have money. We are all friends. Don't treat us like strangers!"I looked at Babbu for support.

"Uhh, yes . . . yes." Babbu was uncomfortable.

"See, even Babbu agrees," I tried to make up for Babbu's lack of enthusiasm.

Sanjay looked at me and smiled warmly. "Arjun, thanks, but that's not what—"

"Not a word from you," I again interrupted him. "By the grace of God, things will again become normal soon. We will definitely talk about money then."

Before Sanjay left our office, I patted him on his back and assured him again that it's a temporary situation from which they will recover in no time. He nodded gratefully and thanked us for everything. I was really happy to feel some positive chemistry between the two of us.

"Is it so bad? Tamanna mentioned it on the phone today, but she did not seem to be that disturbed." Sangini was surprised and confused when I told her about Sanjay's condition over dinner.

"She probably didn't want to worry you," I said.

"Yeah, maybe. Or maybe Sanjay didn't tell her about it properly . . ." Sangini trailed off. She had unintentionally entered an awkward territory. Her remark reminded me of all those years when I had hidden our true financial status from her.

"Do you think there's enough salt in the dal?" she quickly diverted the topic.

"Uhh . . . hmm, yeah," I mumbled.

Later that night, I found myself struggling to stop my mind from going into the Tamanna zone. I repeatedly reminded myself of Sanjay's problem, his troubled face, and the faith he had placed in me. I chanted, *Sanjay is in deep trouble, Sanjay needs my support, Sanjay trusts me, Sanjay is Tamanna's husband.*

***

The next day, I didn't take my usual detour to pass by Tamanna's house. Today, more than ever, I was sincerely trying to think of Tamanna as *Sanjay's wife* and of Sanjay as my friend and not a necessary evil that came with Tamanna.

Before getting out of the car, I sent an encouraging good-morning message to Sanjay. He replied with a *"Thnx so much buddy"* within a minute. In the office too, I earnestly tried to concentrate on Sanjay's project. Around midday, he called up Babbu regarding some additions to the website. The additions were not many, but all of them required a large amount of effort. Babbu gave the necessary directions to our software engineer and designers after briefly discussing them with me.

Later, I finished a major task and wanted a break. My first thought was that I must open Tamanna's collage and feast my eyes for a while. But I rejected the idea immediately. The next thought was that I should go through my verses for her for some time. It took me some seconds to get over that too. Finally, I decided to just take a walk. I got up and walked to the cabin door. But then . . . I gave in to my craving. All my control vanished into thin air. I almost ran back to my desk, and before my conscience could stop me, I opened the folder and read all seventeen of them again. By the time I finished, I was again awash with my love for Tamanna. She was no longer *Sanjay's wife*; she was again *my Tamanna. My precious, precious Tamanna.*

***

Some days later, Sanjay visited our office for an update meeting. He still looked down and demoralised. He informed us that he had started going to his Gurgaon office and that he had introduced another partner in the project, who would bring funds to the company at that critical juncture. He promised us some audio-visual work for a company that, it seemed, he had not even started.

When his phone rang in the middle of the meeting, he went out to receive it. Before he picked it up though, I saw that it said *Wife Calling*. I was really confused by that. For more than two weeks now, I had been in regular touch with him. I had sent him dozens of inspiring messages. I had thought that we had covered a lot of ground in our friendship. There was no reason for him to go out to talk to Tamanna. With some difficulty, I discounted his behaviour as his nature.

When the meeting ended, I expected him to mention our pending bills or at least ask me about a possible dinner get-together. But he didn't talk about either money or socialising. We had not had a single dinner together in more than a month, and our pending payments had crossed seventy thousand rupees. I was not in a position to ask or mention anything myself. After all, how could you talk about partying and payments with a friend who is going through a financial crunch?

After Sanjay left, Babbu went back to work quietly, which was unusual. After any meeting, he always came to my desk to discuss it. Clearly, he was annoyed because of the whole silence over our unpaid bills. I prayed for a change in Sanjay's financial position, so that he could give our money to us.

For some time, I had been hiding the project details from Sangini. She had no idea that the project size had now increased manifold and that Sanjay had not paid us anything apart from the seven thousand he'd shelled out in the beginning. I had not brought it up even during my infrequent conversations with Tamanna. Maybe I did not want any negativity to appear in our relationship. So all we spoke about was my book and my writing. I took care to keep our conversations short because I was afraid too much of talking with her might make me confess my love to her. Talking to the very girl for whom I had been composing love verses was like riding a see-saw with my secret in my lap.

One day, almost involuntarily, I started editing my verses and creating a book of poetry out of them. I started proofreading the language and correcting the flow of each verse. Even as I started, I scolded myself: *A book of your own love verses? Wake up, Arjun, wake up. You are headed towards disaster. Have you gone mad?*

But, these thoughts served only to postpone the editing by a few minutes. Because, after that, the hurricane of my desire silenced my rational mind and I got down to work. Within three days, I had written the preface for the poetry collection.

When Babbu saw what I was up to, he said, "This is such a historical moment in my life. For the first time, I am witnessing a man create such a unique time bomb for his own destruction."

***

Some days later, Sanjay posted an album on Facebook that shocked me. It had pictures of his and his brother's families happily holidaying in the Radisson Blu Hotel, Goa. From nobody's face did it appear that they were in financial trouble. This upset me for three reasons: First, Tamanna was away, and Delhi suddenly felt lonely to me. Second, neither Tamanna nor Sanjay had ever told me they were going on a trip. And third, the baby elephant had the money to party with his brother in a five-star hotel but no money to pay our bills.

"It is because of your stupid love that we are in such a position. Otherwise, we would have earned at least a lakh by now," Babbu blew up when he saw the pictures. "This leech can never change. I had long ago sensed that he is screwing us, but I had to keep quiet because of your compassion towards your girlfriend's husband! Bastard is enjoying in Goa and here in our office he comes wearing torn clothes. Bloody liar!"

Before I could say anything, he stormed out of the room. I kept looking at the pictures for some time. They seemed like a betrayal to me. I had been supporting and helping Sanjay so much. I deserved a better treatment from him. Then suddenly it occurred to me that pictures could lie. Maybe we were jumping to the wrong conclusions.

When I casually mentioned the trip to Sangini, she was not surprised. In fact, she already knew about it and was pretty normal about the whole thing. As we spoke over dinner, I got three missed-call alerts from Airtel. All three were from Tamanna and had been made forty-eight hours earlier. Again, I was furious with the company. My Tamanna probably tried calling me to inform me about the trip, but due to the technological malfunction, she could not reach me.

Gosh! Couldn't she send me one stray SMS instead? . . . Well, maybe she wanted to speak to me before going. May be an SMS would not have done justice. Yes, maybe . . .

For the next seven days, Facebook was my best buddy. Sanjay kept updating the album and I kept downloading Tamanna's breathtaking pictures from it. Most of the time, they were seen in the swimming pool or at the beach, with Tamanna wearing revealing outfits and getting cosy with Sanjay. But that did not make me feel jealous. My love was my love, and nobody could affect that.

Finally, the family came back; Tamanna was back. I learned this through Sangini. She had got a call from Tamanna. That again upset me, because she had not called me. I kept checking my phone again and again, thinking I would receive a call. And guess what? I did!

I had barely said a hello when Tamanna shouted out everything in one go, "Sorrrryyyyyyy! We couldn't talk before going. You know it was so sudden and so surprising for us. Sanjay's brother had planned it without even telling us. I had to rush with my sis-in-law for some very essential shopping for all of us. But I did call you a couple of times, and all the time your phone was not reachable. So, sir, it was your fault and not mine!"

All my anger and unhappiness vanished instantly. As she

shared the general details of the trip, we laughed together. Everything was normal and friendly again. Once, towards the end, I was on the verge of enquiring about their financial situation, but stopped. That would have been an absolutely unmanly act. I thought that if I had a problem with Sanjay, I ought to clarify it with him instead of seeking answers from his wife.

Two days later, Sanjay visited our office, looking much better. "To avoid depression, my brother had organised this trip, and I could not say no to him," he explained. "It was good for the entire family."

My phone buzzed. It was Babbu's SMS: *Tell this bastard to pay for the project.* He was sitting right in front of me. I ignored the text. Babbu grew restless and went out.

"First month will be very crucial for all of us," Sanjay was saying. "Be ready for the big jump, buddy."

I waited for him to mention the pending payment, but he did not say anything on that topic. Babbu had perhaps left for the day from outside only.

"Uhh, perhaps he had some urgent work," I explained his disappearance to Sanjay as I walked out with him.

When the cool breeze touched my cheeks outside, a new poem started forming in my mind. I walked Sanjay to his car, and throughout the way, my mind kept creating a new love verse for his wife.

22

A week later, Sanjay paid us a surprise visit at the office, looking terribly disturbed. He told us that the new partner who was to invest funds in the project had suddenly disappeared. Now he was planning to start a new company for incense sticks and handicrafts exports together with his brother. Humbly, he requested us to create a new website to promote the incense stick venture in Finland. I mentally calculated the money involved. If we took up the project, it would cost us not less than fifty thousand rupees.

"I don't know why God is taking such a test. Guys, please help."

To my surprise, it was Babbu who took the baton. "Sure, we are there for you," he said sweetly. "But . . . Sanjay . . . as you must already know, your current project has already become much bigger than what we had calculated. So, if you could , I mean, pay some—"

Sanjay cut him short. "Oh, yes, of course! So sorry, I was just going to mention it. I, well, okay, you tell me the full amount till date and I will clear your payments by day after tomorrow." He smiled reassuringly.

That took both Babbu and me by surprise. We looked at each other and smiled. We had wrongly judged this man. He was not trying to fool us. I felt guilty for doubting him.

After he left, I politely asked Babbu to create a bill of the exact amount we had spent on the project. I didn't want to include any profit in it. Surprisingly, Babbu agreed readily. Maybe he did it for the sake of our friendship and my love, or maybe he was as touched by Sanjay's situation and response as I was. Or maybe he saw it as an opportunity to earn bigger profits later. But, the good news was that at the end of the day, he created a bill for 1.30 lakh rupees, the whole sum we had invested in his project. Sanjay agreed to the figure without any questions and even offered to give a post-dated cheque. We vehemently turned down that offer and Babbu got busy making the Finland project with our techie.

***

Ten days went by without any sort of payment from Sanjay. Twice, he called up on his own to apologise for the delay. He said he was terribly busy. We bought his excuses apprehensively and kept waiting.

Meanwhile, I had started imitating Tamanna. A number of times, I would smile like her, eat like her, and even try to walk like her. In this way, I felt I could keep her with me every second of the day. By now, I had also created the front cover design of my book of verses.

Five more days passed. There was still no trace of any payment from the baby elephant. For the last two days, he had not even returned my calls. I became tense again and thought of talking to Tamanna about this matter. But my heart stopped me every time. It wasn't ready to initiate any negative conversation with her. I considered my little world with her totally different from the negative realities of outside. It was a world where people like Sanjay had no place.

When I rang Sanjay the next day, he picked up the call, much to my relief, but he sounded very sad. When I enquired, he admitted being very upset but refused to divulge anything more than: "professionally, this is the roughest patch of my life." Worried, I offered to come down with Sangini to meet him and Tamanna that evening. He agreed to it, but very reluctantly. I said I would confirm the time around 6 p.m., and we hung up.

After discussing with Sangini, I messaged him from my mobile at 5.30 p.m. to confirm the meeting. But he didn't respond. When I called him an hour later, he didn't pick up his phone. It was at 8 p.m. that he finally messaged: *Yes, u may come.* That was very formal. But we went anyway.

It proved to be a short, strange meeting. His brother and his family were not around. They were at the mall, Sanjay said. We generally chitchatted for a while. Then Tamanna and Sangini moved to the kitchen to get dinner. With the women gone, I asked him what had happened. He said it was very embarrassing to explain it to "just anyone"—as if I was a stranger to him, as if we had not known each other for three years! When I insisted, he said, "We all go through rough patches professionally . . . it happens all the times, hmmm . . . Could we talk about something better please?"

Throughout the meeting, Tamanna looked completely normal. From her behaviour, it did not appear that anything at all was wrong in the family. And Sangini did not bring up the project. She knew that Sanjay had become our client; yet she did not say a word about it. When I look back, I feel that it was as if some higher power designed that meeting so that what eventually happened in the weeks following it could happen.

All in all, what I was hoping would be a pep talk and catch-up meeting ended up being only a general chat about our education system and how useless it had become for the current breed of school students. Sanjay barely participated in the conversation and I was too mentally preoccupied to say much either. I was happy to meet and see Tamanna, but at the same time, I could feel that a bleak future awaited our relationship, and the person responsible for it would be Sanjay. A strange fear settled deep inside me somewhere.

"Is there something that I need to know, Arjun?" Sangini asked concernedly on our way back home. "Is your project going okay?"

I had not told her anything about the worrying financial details of the project. Even now, I did not want to say anything. It was as if I was waiting for something to happen—a forthcoming event that would reveal the truth to me. So I lied. "Everything is okay, sweetheart! Trust me."

She stared at me for a while before looking away. It made me nervous. We didn't talk for the rest of the drive back home.

When I reached office the next day, I found out from our designer that Babbu had gone to meet Simmi. Before leaving, he had instructed that all further work on the Finland project be stopped, even though it was almost 90% complete.

***

For the next four days, there was no word from Sanjay. Though Tamanna's physical proximity was no more important to me, I still greatly wanted her in my life. I wanted to be able to call her up from time to time and hear her voice and laughter for the rest of my life.

So, still maintaining substantial faith in Sanjay's new-found friendship, I did what I would always remember as sheer stupidity. Over the next few days, I literally put my dignity and my own happiness on stake to provide help to a person who never ever deserved even an iota of it. My own clothes were torn apart, and I was trying to give shelter to his well-clothed being. This was not big-heartedness but stupidity of the highest degree.

Five days had gone by since we met as families. After the day's work, I was now busy with the editing of my verse book. Babbu was now normal and had told me clearly that he would not raise any topic of that "bastard." According to him bygones were bygones. Though he knew about my editing of the book, he always only reacted with a smile and a stray comment, saying, "You are a gone case . . . screwing your life for that bastard's wife."

In all those five days I never got even a stray SMS from Sanjay. This time I wanted to be patient with my observation.

At about 6.30 p.m. the same day, I felt an unusually strong urge to speak to Sanjay. His sad face was there in front of my eyes. It was as if I could hear his grief-stricken voice. That was strange. I tried to ignore it, but within minutes the urge touched enormous magnitude.

What's happening to me? I think with Tamanna's love I am truly losing my normal senses. Unable to stop my mysterious desire, I finally called up Sanjay.

That day, something that I had never imagined possible happened: Sanjay cried on the phone. He revealed that the financial problems of the family had aggravated further. Some more bungling had been unearthed in his brother's business and a major crisis had hit his school as well. One of their teachers had allegedly misbehaved with a student and his parents had filed a case against them. Consequently, some teachers had left the school mid-session.

Sanjay sounded disillusioned and hopeless and my heart went out to him. For years I had felt the same pain, shed the same tears. I knew that a man's tears were his ultimate expression of pain. I heard him out patiently and said soothing, encouraging words. The conversation left me highly disturbed. All the memories of my past came back to haunt me. At home, I remained quiet and withdrawn. Over dinner, Sangini told me that she had spoken to Tamanna earlier that day to plan a dinner get-together. But Tamanna had refused the invitation, saying that they were busy with the relatives from Finland. Sangini didn't seem to know anything about the troubles at Sanjay's school. Which meant that either Tamanna did not tell her or she herself did not know. I suspected it was the latter. I wanted to believe that Sanjay was doing with Tamanna what I had done with Sangini—hiding his financial failures from his wife.

The next day, I got a call from Sanjay early in the morning. He said he was in an urgent need of funds. He wanted to take a loan of about fifty lakh and requested me to help him with it. I had several contacts in the banking and loan sectors and had taken many loans in my life. I told Sanjay about this and assured him I'd be glad to help him. I asked him to come down to the office with his documents to discuss things further.

Fortunately, Babbu was again out with Simmi that day. If he had met Sanjay and heard his request, he would have surely created a scene. Sanjay arrived around midday, looking shaky and broken. I felt really sorry for him. I felt like he was a person about whom I had repeatedly gone wrong. He was carrying a heavy bunch of papers. They were the documents of his brother's India branch office in Connaught Place. Before seeing the papers I had had no idea that they had an office in CP. When I asked him about it, he said it was a small place with only two employees.

I promised to help him with the loans. I wanted to talk to him about our payment but then how could I have asked a person who had come to me for help to get a loan to pay outstanding bills? I remained quiet and reassured him about a positive outcome.

***

For the next several weeks, I spoke to anybody and everybody I knew from the loan departments of various banks about Sanjay's requirement. I photocopied at least twenty sets of documents at my cost and distributed it to everyone I knew in the circle. I lost count of the number of offices I personally visited for this job. I left no stone unturned so that his loan could be sanctioned. I prayed for him daily. Many a time, I felt as if I was putting my own dignity at stake by virtually folding my hands and requesting people to help. Due to my intense efforts, the loan agents started thinking that I had some vested interest in the matter.

But my efforts were of no use. I received a similar response from every quarter—the documents had no strength. Some said that the company's financials were too weak. Others claimed that the company was fabricated. When I shared this with Sanjay, he loudly debunked these "disgusting theories." In the initial days, he would call me twice every day for updates. But when he sensed that I was unlikely to be of any help, he stopped calling. And if I called, his tone would be dry and bored.

All through this time, Babbu mostly maintained a stoic silence, which spoke louder than anything he had ever said. But one day, when I really prodded him to share his views, he had merely this to say, "Once a bastard, always a bastard. Total fraud motherfucker. You focus on having a wonderful time with his wife, please. He deserves that only."

Another day, when I returned to the office after a meeting with a bank agent (I had skipped lunch for that), he welcomed me with these words, "Oh God! Just for that girl you have literally become an office peon? Oh my God! You are even ready to lose your self-respect, isn't it? In your own shaky financial state, you are spending money on petrol for going to loan offices for that bastard. Why? Only for that girl? DAMN YOU, MAN!"

I didn't respond to any of his comments. I knew he was right in his own way, but he didn't understand so much more—sacrifice, pain, failure . . . love.

Meanwhile, I kept composing verses and editing and polishing my book. That was the only activity that gave me any peace. By now, I had created thirty-six verses and done the page setting and designing. Soon I found myself taking a printout of the final copy. A strange happiness emerged from the bottom of my heart as I took the printed pages in my trembling hands for the first time. I sent them to a stationer for spiral binding. When I got the final bound copy in my hand, I took it in my arms and held it to my chest. I caressed and smelled the pages. It was a precious creation of my mine. It was an exquisite evidence of my true, untainted love for Tamanna.

After that day, I started experiencing sudden bouts of madness—bouts of craving to see Tamanna at any cost. But alas, I was unable to do so. I could only call her, and I did that thrice in the next ten days. Each time, she would encourage me to write my book, and then would quickly but apologetically disconnect, saying she was busy with Sanjay's brother's family.

I wish I could tell her that while she was busy shopping and eating and gossiping with her relatives, I had created a veritable testament of my love for her. I genuinely wondered if it would

ever be possible for me to show the book to her . . . even
though I knew the tragic answer in my heart—that book would
always remain the biggest secret of my life.

23

I overlooked, ignored, and tolerated everything that Sanjay did because I didn't want things to become bitter between the two of us. If I had behaved even a little strictly or roughly with him, there was a real possibility that my friendship with his wife would have ended. So I turned a blind eye every time he lied to me or used me. Despite everything he did, I tried to be in touch with him by sending him inspirational messages and calling every now and then. Steadily, he got back to his old tone and behaviour. All the humbleness and politeness he had shown when he required our help disappeared. But I persevered. I threw my dignity to the dogs because of my love for Tamanna.

I also carried my book of verses everywhere I went, be it to meetings or business lunches. For me, it was a sacred epic. My hands would tremble, my eyes would blink continuously, and goosebumps would erupt on my skin each time I touched my book.

***

One day, I was lost in my thoughts about how to start writing my new book when the Love Goddess knocked the door of my mobile phone. It was after a long time that she was calling me to talk. For months now, it was mostly me who would call her and she who would quickly disconnect the call. So now, suddenly seeing her incoming call was like a gift from the heavens for me.

"Hey, Tamanna, how are you?" I started off.

"I am good, Arjun. But you don't sound very well. What's up?" she asked, concerned. "Why do I always feel that you are in some sort of constant delusion?"

My heart skipped a beat. *It takes her only a sentence from me to know how I am feeling. We are deeply connected, she and I. Something very strong from within my being touches her heart all the time.* I took the book of my life in my hand and fumbled a response. "I-I don't know . . . really. B-b-but I . . ."

Hearing my broken reply, she chuckled and, then, sighed. Her deep breath touched my ears. In a flash of a second, a volcanic madness of emotions erupted from deep within me and I let go. "Tamanna, it is love that touches a human heart. It is love that is the basis of this wonderful life. It is love that is the most sacred thing in the world. Tamanna, I have decided. I want to write a wonderful love story." My eyes welled up.

At that, Tamanna chuckled again. Her voice, her breath, and her joy were touching my ears and kissing my soul. I held my verse book in my hand as tightly as I could.

"All right, sir, then fall in love and write your love story. It would be a masterpiece, I bet it," she jokingly said and laughed.

Sweat trickled from the palm that was holding my book. My senses had greatly weakened. I forgot my commitment to keep my love inside my heart. A strange force pushed the words up my throat. In my state of immense happiness, I laughed and responded, "Okay, then, let's do it."

She inhaled sharply, and I came back to my senses, and she

laughed it off. "I think that is kind of going a little overboard, isn't it?"

Before I could respond, the door bell played spoilsport. The call had to be terminated immediately.

***

One week later, when I logged into Facebook at work for updates, my wall gave me a jolt. Sanjay and his brother were on a family holiday yet again, this time to Singapore! They had uploaded pictures of themselves at the airport and at the hotel.

How can he be so shameless? I was disgusted and hurt. *He has the moolah to travel internationally, but no money to pay us? This is ridiculous.*

To my ill luck, Babbu entered the room just then and saw the pictures. He moved closer to the screen.

"This is again one of the costliest hotels in Singapore where this bastard is staying." He paused for a moment, shaking his head. Then he shouted, "HE IS SUCH A CHEAT!"

In the coming days, more pictures were uploaded by Sanjay. The trip was not limited to Singapore. They went to Malaysia and Thailand too. It was a good twenty-day trip. I downloaded all the photos with Tamanna in them. By now, I had collected more than fifty pictures of hers and had two collages, one with her in Indian clothes and another in Western outfits.

When Sanjay finally updated, *Back to Delhi frm a tiring holiday,* I thought of calling him, but the very thought gave me immensely negative vibes. So I postponed the call to the next day and then to the next. Finally, I called him after two days of their return. Sanjay's tone was somewhat dry. I enquired about his general well being.

"I am absolutely fine, dude. You tell me."

"So . . ." I hesitated. "You didn't even tell me about the trip . . ."

His response was like a whiplash. "Hey, I didn't know informing you in advance was mentioned in the contract. Sorry."

In a flash of a second, my whole being got filled with negativity and anger. It was terrible. I felt like slamming the phone down. But just then, Sanjay spoke up in a gentler tone, "Actually I am in the service of my brother these days. It was on his behest that we all agreed."

He was clearly lying. I was losing my temper. Taking a deep breath, I said, "You haven't even checked the work we've done. The entire project is almost finished."

"Oh come on, dude. I checked the website you created many times. The home page is still incomplete. I had asked for some email IDs from Babbu. He still hasn't created them. Even some links on the home page are non-functional." His tone was rude and taunting.

I had no idea about all these problems. I had not checked the work myself. But his manner of speaking completely shook me. I had to terminate the call on the pretext of some pending work.

When I asked Babbu about the validity of his claims, he got mad. "HE IS THE WORST SUCKER I HAVE EVER SEEN! Bastard wants to get work worth lakhs of rupees done in seven thousand only."

Usually, Babbu stopped after one remark, but that day he bulldozed on.

"Tell me, did the sucker even say a small thanks to you for all the fucking efforts you put in for his loan thing? For his fraud company, you made yourself a laughing stock in your circle. For his thankless work, you went to so many offices, countless pages you got photocopied. Why?" He was almost screaming now. "That BASTARD was using you all the time. And in doing that, he used our company as well."

I remained quiet and listened. Babbu was speaking the truth. The bitter truth I had been trying to avoid for a long time. But even so, somewhere in my mind, I was still creating verses.

"Just to impress your girlfriend and have a good time with her, you sold your self- esteem in the market. You became a servant to the dog."

I could not keep quiet any longer. "Babbu," I said softly. "Please, I request you, don't use wrong words for Tamanna. It's obvious you can't understand even a tiny bit of my love, so please—"

"EXTRA-MARITAL-AFFAIR," Babbu bellowed, thumping the table. "That is what it is! Because of your affair, we have lost our money. You have faced disgrace all your life, but still you haven't learnt anything." With that, Babbu stormed out of the office.

This was the first time that Babbu had spoken to me in such a way. I was completely shaken. My mind was numb. I knew I was wrong. But even then Tamanna was never my girlfriend. I had never thought of her like that.

Just then, Babbu entered the cabin again, walked up to my table, looked into my eyes, and, softly but firmly, said, "Our web designer's salary for this month is still pending. Call your girlfriend and tell her about the bastard. She will definitely heed to your request and ask her scoundrel husband to pay up."

We held each other's gaze for a second, before I nodded faintly and Babbu strode out again.

That day, I took my book home for the first time, carefully hidden in my bag. I was feeling very lonely. There was nobody on earth who could understand my situation, it seemed.

Happy and Babbu's understanding of what I felt was crude and superficial. The whole night, I did not sleep. Instead, I kept reading my love epic over and over again and thinking about Tamanna and all the conversations we had had. By next morning, I must have read my verses at least fifty times.

Filled with anger and emotions, I called up Sanjay at 9.30 a.m. As usual, his accent was dry. I enquired about his brother's financial condition and the loan.

"Nothing is working out as of now," he responded casually. "Things are still very tense . . . let's see!"

Then, summoning my patience and courage, I initiated the real conversation. I plainly informed him about the ready advertising website and the continuing work for project Finland. I never said anything about the payments however.

"Hey! Hey! Hey, dude, relax!" I felt like I had a big mistake by ringing him up. My last remaining shreds of self-esteem were on stake. "Don't run so fast, man. Let me first check everything. Things have been very rough at my end. I am struggling to stabilise myself. I did not get time to check anything thoroughly. Give me some time at least." He paused for a second, then added, "Google is anyway offering websites for free." Saying that, he chuckled, in order to apply some honey over the indecent comment.

My blood boiled. Yet, I controlled my temper. Very softly I said, "Sanjay, don't misunderstand me, please. All I was saying was that your project is ready."

"No, I am not misunderstanding anything, dude. It is you who is trying to remind me of something else."

That was enough for me. My instincts told me that the conversation was about to turn nasty. Sanjay was a dirt bag and I would only soil my hands by arguing with him. So, in haste, I terminated the call.

For a long time, I remained seated inside the cabin, not doing anything. I was blank. I felt like my life was being uprooted right in front of my eyes and I was not able to do anything about it.

24

It had been two hours since my phone call to Sanjay. I was sitting in the office. Babbu had taken the day off. He was probably too pissed with me. His words from our fight yesterday were still ringing in my ears.

Because of your affair, we have lost our money. You have faced disgrace all your life, but still you haven't learnt anything . . . Our web designer's salary for this month is still pending. Call your girlfriend and tell her about the bastard.

Maybe I should call Tamanna and discuss this, I thought. She was my friend. We shared a deep bond. And it was my responsibility to inform her about her highly immoral husband.

In that delusional state of mind, I dialled her number.

"Hey, Mr. Author, what's up?" She sounded excited as usual. I heard her and half my psyche was healed.

I must share with her something special today, I thought. A line of poetry walked into my mind. "I think about you, dear Tamanna, all the time; you're an eternal friend, a special friend, a mirror of my life."

I held my breath, waiting for Tamanna's response. She took a moment and then burst out laughing. I heaved a sigh of relief and started laughing too. Soon we were laughing in rhythm, in perfect synchronisation. It was as if we had created a language of laughter, and through it our hearts were talking. My heart spoke, hers listened. That moment penetrated deep into my soul.

I had totally surprised myself by saying that. Maybe the verse was nothing in comparison to what I had written in my book. But the fact that my mind had created poetry and had presented it to the person for whom it was intended made my little verse very special. My voice had touched her ears and had travelled right to her heart. And to be able to utter "Dear Tamanna" was like being in seventh heaven for me.

"Oh God, oh my God, Arjun, I am deeply honoured. I don't know what to say."

Tamanna, Tamanna, do you know what's happening to me? Tamanna, please help me, my dear. You stay deep inside me, always. See what I have created for you, my dear Tamanna.

I took my book in my sweaty palms and suddenly lost all inhibitions. "Tamanna, I . . . I want to tell you something . . . something that is connected to—"

"Oh, Arjun, there's a call waiting on my phone," she interrupted me. "It is Sanjay. Just wait, I will call back." She hung up.

Sanjay's name brought me back to the real world. The truth of my love had been on the tip of my tongue! In that extremely weak moment, I was about to do something that I'd always thought I'd never do. In the two minutes Tamanna took to call back, I gained a better control of my senses.

"Some of his friends are coming today for dinner, some new acquaintances," Tamanna said when she called back. "So, I got the order to prepare dinner accordingly."

I disliked that Sanjay had *ordered* Tamanna. I detested that he was throwing a party when he couldn't afford to even pay us. And I hated that he was having dinner with his new acquaintances but had no time for us. Anger surged inside me.

After a pause, Tamanna continued, hesitating, "Hmmm, Arjun, I didn't tell Sanjay I was talking to you. So please don't tell him about our conversation if by chance you speak to him."

Today was the first time that such a mention had taken place in our conversation. I already had a sharp pin named Sanjay deep in my heart. In a flash of a second my anger flared up like blazing fire in a jungle. "Does that mean you've told him about our previous phone calls?" I asked.

"Whaaat . . .?" She fumbled. "What do you mean by that? Of course I tell him."

That made me *mad* with rage. I forgot all my commitments to myself, I forgot how precarious my position was, I forgot that I had vowed to never cross lines. Most of all, I forgot that some careless words from my end was all it would take for the beautiful and delicate secret universe I had created with my Tamanna to shatter to a million pieces.

"Huhh? Sorry, I don't believe you. A man like him is not even remotely capable of understanding our relationship." I paused as waves of fury lashed inside me. Then, in a tone that was brimming with anger, I said the words that changed my life. "I think we should end this bloody drama today itself. Hiding from a man like him is most disgraceful for me."

There was a long pause. Neither of us said anything. The world came to a standstill. The only sound was that of our breathing. Then, after what seemed like an eternity to me, she said, "What drama, Arjun? What are you saying? What have I done, Arjun?" She started crying.

That brought me crashing back down to earth. My whole body was shaking. I could see my hands trembling badly.

Oh my God, no, Arjun, no! This is Tamanna, the love of your life. She is crying because of you.

My mind went completely numb. Frantically, I tried to

think of some comforting words to say to her. But before I could speak, the damned mobile signal played spoilsport and the call got disconnected.

Fuck you, Airtel people. We will forever remain a third-world country!

I immediately redialled her number. But it was switched off. I dialled again after two minutes. It was still switched off. Maybe Airtel was not to be blamed. Maybe she had disconnected the call out of anger and switched off her phone. I kept redialling.

It was 12.15 p.m. Half an hour had passed. By now I had tried her phone over fifty times. Tamanna . . . the Tamanna of my dreams, of my book, was angry. Life, for me, had taken a complete U-turn. I had never thought such a day would come.

Slowly, my thinking capacities started diminishing.

At 1.15 p.m., her phone was still switched off. My mind was almost frozen. I was losing the sense of where I was sitting or even what I was doing and why I was doing it. Occasionally, my hands flew to my face to wipe away the tears that constantly flowed down from my eyes.

Another hour rolled away. She was yet to switch on her phone and I had not moved even an inch from my chair. Somebody opened the door of our cabin. It was Babbu. I slowly looked towards him.

"Gosh, man, what happened? You are crying!" He pulled open the table drawer, took out some tissues, and gave them to me. I took them mechanically, but didn't do anything with them.

"Arjun, *yaar*, what happened? Tell me, please!"

Controlling myself, I tried to speak, but could not utter a single word. Instead I started sobbing.

"Hey, come on, Arjun, control yourself, you are a grown-up man. Control yourself please. Tell me what happened!" Babbu was visibly worried.

It took me a while to stop crying. Then I told Babbu what had happened.

Babbu heard everything patiently. After I was done speaking, he sighed, his gaze downcast. He seemed to be calculating the appropriate words for his response.

"It is my fault entirely . . ." he began after a long pause.

"Wha—" I had barely completed the word when he raised his hand, indicating me to stay quiet.

"If I had not said those harsh words to you, you wouldn't have become so negative about Sanjay and wouldn't have said anything to Tamanna."

To an extent, Babbu was correct. But I didn't react. My mind was with Tamanna. The eagerness to make everything normal again was gaining maddening proportions inside my heart.

Babbu continued to be highly apologetic. He remained quiet for some time, thinking. Then: "Arjun, I never knew that Tamanna meant so much to you. I am shaken seeing you like this. If her anger can shatter you like this, then I can now finally imagine what she is for you and what you actually feel for her. I am not a wise man like you, and so my words may not be that great—"

"Uh . . . no Babbu . . ." I managed, but Babbu would have none of it. He stood up from his chair and squatted in front of me. "She really means something to you . . . I am sorry, brother, I am sorry. But don't worry. She will be okay soon, she will be okay."

These were the kindest words Babbu had ever said to me. In normal circumstances, I would have felt warm and grateful for them. But at that moment, the sadness of angering Tamanna was strangulating me.

Two hours later, at 4.15 p.m., Tamanna's phone was still

switched off. Babbu had tried to take me out of the office twice, but in vain. I preferred the balcony near the staircase instead. It remained vacant most of the time. I hadn't eaten anything since the tragic phone call. Everything seemed a waste to me. Just then my phone rang.

It was Tamanna calling. I giggled in sheer happiness and came back to my senses. The happiness I felt was of an unimaginable magnitude.

"Hi Arjun." Her tone, as expected, was serious. "Sorry, my phone ran out of battery. I was about to charge it when my mother came over to the house unannounced. So . . . I just didn't get the time to talk."

Oh Tamanna . . . thanks sooooo much . . . thanks so much for calling.

My emotions were too overwhelmingly intense to be contained today. I broke all the barriers and all the guards I had built over the last three years and poured my heart out. I had upset her and now I had to make amends. Without thinking anything further, I spoke and just spoke. And she simply listened.

"Tamanna . . . uhh . . . you c-c-came into my life when I was going through a rough patch. Ta-Ta-Tamanna, you met me and I formed a mystical friendship with you. I-I-I respect you immensely, Tamanna. Dear Tamanna, you are a dear friend to me . . . you-you-you are the friend for whom I have been waiting all my life. Forgive me, forgive me, please. Somehow, your presence in my life gives me immense comfort and assurance . . . oh please . . . please forgive me. You came at a time when I needed maximum encouragement and support. You-you encouraged the writer in me, Tamanna . . . Ta-Ta-Tamanna, you pulled my sagging confidence . . . no, no . . . not even in my wildest dreams had I thought this would happen,

Tamanna. No, Tamanna . . . no . . . no . . . no . . . Don't think wrong. I value Sangini greatly . . . I love her. . . but I remain so so so confused . . . so confused all the time. I remain so confused, Tamanna. I have great respect for you . . . and-and-and I have always tried to be a sincere friend to Sanjay as well . . . You . . . I . . . I mean . . . I have . . . please, Tamanna, please," I pleaded like a child, "please, don't be angry with me. I-I can never ever intend to hurt you. Please . . . please . . . don't . . . don't be . . ."

"What are you doing, Arjun?"

"No, please let me speak today . . . I never intended to hurt you. I can never ever think of causing you any trouble. You have no idea of what you are for . . . for me. Listen carefully, Tamanna . . . I know Sanjay is my friend. Every time I called you, I had this truth in my mind that Sanjay is my friend and you are his wife. But what do I do if I feel closer to you? I could never gel well with him. I tried many times but . . . but it never happened. Many times I felt guilty that I am talking to Sanjay's wife. But . . . you met me at a time in my life when I had darkness all around. You inspired me. Your presence gave me happiness. Even though you were not doing anything consciously, I felt boundless joy whenever I saw you.

"Though we hardly spoke for months, I had imagined how you would be in my mind. And when we started talking . . . you turned out to be just the same. I always felt a great connection with you. But please, please, please, for God's sake, I assure you that I never had wrong feelings for you.

"You are like an angel to me. I respect you, Tamanna. I can never express in words the respect and regard that I have for you. Life has taken painful tests and I am courageously fighting. You have an important place in my life, as . . . as a friend. But I was little upset with Sanjay . . . and you suddenly took his name and . . ."

"What about Sanjay?"

That was a wonderful opportunity for me to narrate the lowly act that Sanjay had done. But my wisdom guided me to stop. My confession would have resulted in tension between husband and wife, and I never wanted that. The matter was between me and Sanjay.

"Uhh . . . nothing much," I replied. "Nothing. Just an argument, nothing important."

She sighed deeply. "Okay, but please . . . control yourself." She sounded better now. It seemed that she had somewhat understood my point of view.

"Sorry, Tamanna," I apologised again and started sobbing.

"Arjun, please . . ."

"You are an angel. An angel. An angel in my life . . . That's my truth." I felt exhausted.

A brief lull followed next. From the other side, I could hear her breathing.

"Arjun . . ." There was no anger in her tone. That was immensely comforting for me.

"Relax please. I am not upset at all. I understand everything. But now I must hang up . . ."

"Yes, sure." Her wish was my command.

After we disconnected, I felt like I was breathing properly for the first time in years. I felt immensely and truly free, as if someone had pulled away the chains that I had been shackled in for months.

My world was back with me.

***

The next day, Babbu and I had to leave for Chandigarh for some business-related work. It was unusually hectic there. For three days, I did not initiate any communication with Tamanna. There were no calls or messages from her side either. I began to get worried.

Babbu assured me that things were normal, that Tamanna would stay in my life like before.

On the fourth day, unable to control my desire, I finally called her early in the morning. She didn't take my call. I assumed she was busy and waited the whole day for her to call back. Each time my phone would ring, my heart would skip a beat. I got more than a dozen calls during the day, but none were from her. So, when we reached our hotel in the evening, I called her again. Twice. Still there was no answer. Crossing my fingers and praying that Sanjay was absent from home, I sent her two SMSes. She never replied.

My heart sank. My fears and stress returned. Babbu was still confident. "She can never go away from you. I bet it," he said.

Next day, I called up many times on her phone, but it just kept ringing. The whole day, I could not take interest in anything else. I felt as if I was on trial and the verdict on my death sentence was awaited.

Seeing me terribly upset, Babbu tried to cheer me up. "Relax, man. She must be busy in something. Everything is okay. Don't you worry."

This irked me to no end. I lost my patience and reacted sharply, "How come you are so confident, idiot? She isn't picking up my fucking calls. How do I not worry!"

Just then, an idea surfaced in my mind. A nasty idea that involved fiddling with somebody's right of not wanting to talk to me. Keeping all my maturity and wisdom on one side, I picked up Babbu's phone and dialled her number. Even before Babbu could figure out my intent, Tamanna picked up the phone.

"It's me. Arjun." I immediately clarified. I felt lowly and cheap, but I had to satisfy my curiosity somehow. "I am sorry I had to call you like this, but you are just not taking my calls. What happened? What?"

"Arjun, listen carefully," her tone was stern and cold, "I don't want to talk about anything. Please do your work and take care of your family. Talking to you won't be possible for me anymore."

"WHAT? Are you kidding?"

Please say you are kidding.

But she was serious. "Please, Arjun, grow up. I don't want to talk about anything."

I was completely rattled. Like a child, I said, "Hey, I said sorry to you that day, didn't I?"

"I don't want to talk about that day at all." There was a sense of finality in her tone that was killing me. "You be in your own world and do your duties. My best wishes are always with you. But talking to you like this will not be possible for me anymore." And she disconnected the call.

I didn't hear her voice ever again.

25

The heavens fell apart.

I tried calling Tamanna many times after that, but she didn't answer. I sent her messages too, requesting her to call back, but she didn't reply. And I did not want to deceive her again by calling from another number.

It felt like death. My mind went numb. Babbu tried to console me, but I could not hear his voice properly.

Babbu suggested I drown my grief in alcohol and brought a bottle of whisky. I refused to drink, but he had five pegs and went to sleep. I couldn't sleep for even a single moment. I remained seated on the sofa the entire night, struggling to think, to frame words and sentences in my mind. I didn't get up to even get a glass of water.

At 9.30 the next morning, Sangini messaged me asking about our departure time. We were to leave for Delhi that day. It took all my energy to send her a reply.

A little while later, Babbu's phone rang, waking him up. It was from a new school in Chandigarh. From the conversation, I could make out that they wanted to meet us regarding some work. After finishing the call, Babbu looked around for me and found me on the sofa. Seeing my condition, he said, "You stay here only. I will go and meet them alone."

The whole day I remained seated on the sofa. Before leaving, Babbu had succeeded in forcing some water down my throat, but not in making me eat anything solid. I called and messaged Tamanna several times. In one of the messages, I even wrote that I was not feeling well, and that she must immediately call me back. But there was not a word from her end.

When Babbu returned at 4.30 p.m., he was shocked to see me sitting in the same position he had left me in. He seated himself in front of me and shook my shoulders. I could see his lips moving but the only sound in my ears was that of whistles. I had forgotten all words. My mind was absolutely blank. I felt very weak, and even as Babbu was shaking me, I fell unconscious.

26

When I next opened my eyes, I found myself in a hospital room. Babbu was sitting next to me; his eyes were red. The moment he saw me awake, a smile broke out on his lips and he rushed out to call the doctor.

When the doctor came, he asked me to lift my limbs one by one. I could do that easily. He asked me some routine questions and informed me that I had been unconscious for about five hours. They had conducted all blood tests and everything was normal. He suspected that I had had a nervous breakdown due to extreme stress.

The doctor was in his early thirties and talked compassionately. He gently told me about the gravity of my depression and asked me to take care.

Soon after the doctor exited, Babbu came near me and remarked, "This was not expected of you, Mr. Arjun Singh. Sangini called two hours back asking for our whereabouts. I told her we'd be in Chandigarh for another day and that you forgot your phone in the hotel and went for urgent photocopies of some documents. You better talk to her."

I did not reply. Instead, I asked for my phone. Babbu pulled it out from his trouser pocket and gave it to me. I swiftly opened the gallery and opened the *Family* folder, which contained pictures of Sangini, Sanghmitra, and my mother—my world. I asked Babbu to go out of the room for a while so that I could do my daily prayer in peace. He smiled and moved out.

Slowly I got up from the bed, folded my hands, and prayed, "Almighty, I am not a sinner. Forgive me if I caused pain to anyone . . ."

***

For many weeks after we returned from Chandigarh, my mental condition remained fragile. The doctor at PGI (the hospital in Chandigarh) had prescribed some medicines which I kept at the office. Sangini could notice something was wrong. When she confronted me about it, I managed to convince her that it was all work-related stress.

I kept waiting for some word from Tamanna, but there was none. I didn't hear anything from Sanjay either. One day, Sangini told me that she had spoken to Tamanna about a family meeting. My heart started pounding. I worried that Tamanna might have mentioned what had happened between the two of us. But Sangini seemed normal, so I judged that she had maintained her silence on that matter. I told her that meetings with the Sahnis would not be possible for some time as there had been a nasty argument between Sanjay and me. I asked Sangini to promise me that she'd never ask me for details. She was hesitant and confused, but relented when I insisted.

Meanwhile, I strengthened my faith more than ever. I needed to get back on my feet quickly. I needed to take care of my mental balance. With the medication and my regular prayers, I somehow managed to keep Tamanna's thoughts at bay.

Tamanna's reaction was still like a sharp pain in my mind. Maybe the outpour of my heart had given her the idea that I was crossing the line and getting into a wrong territory of human relations. And that only forced her to take that harsh step. She might have thought that her continued communication might give wrong indications to me, and due to that she reacted so sharply. What more could I think in such hopeless circumstance other than going with my wisdom and provide much needed respite to my pained heart?

But there were times when my heart pained awfully. Many times I felt dejected. I felt low. I had now no courage left to read the book of my love verses. Even touching it would push me towards depression. I explained to myself that my confession to Tamanna had probably given her the impression that I desired her physically. This was why she was not talking to me. But such explanations only served to make me desire to call her up and explain that my love had always been chaste and true.

Babbu communicated with Sanjay twice after we came back. The second time, he got into an argument.

"You owe us 1.30 lakhs. This includes only the basic charges," Babbu told Sanjay clearly.

To his utter shock, he got a shameless reply from Sanjay, "Dude, don't try to cheat me. Google offers websites for free."

Babbu slammed the phone down. We never heard from Sanjay again. Of course, there were no payments from his end either.

***

Two months went by. I was now much better. My persistent prayers and the doctor's medicines had helped me control my emotions and feelings.

Sometimes, though, I lost control. This happened especially

when I was alone. When there would be no one around me, I would secretly talk to Tamanna in my mind. I'd eat with her, discuss my day-to-day routine with her, and walk and talk like her. I would tell her, in my thoughts, *'Look, just have a look at this book. Have a look at the verses, my love.'*

Partings should never be painful. But they are always painful!

Sometimes a maddening craving would erupt in my heart to tell Tamanna that I had no wrong intentions towards her. There was so much inside me. But I could do nothing. All I could do was pray and pop pills. I could not afford another nervous breakdown.

One day, Sangini shared something about Tamanna. She had called Sangini and told her about their forthcoming Finland trip. Sanjay was about to setup some new business along with his brother in that country. Sangini asked me to call up Tamanna.

I nodded.

I had another breakdown soon after that.

And that was when I started writing this book you are holding in your hand.

SANGINI SPEAKS

It was an ordinary summer day of 2012. I had woken up a little late than usual as Sanghmitra's summer vacations were on and Arjun was in Chandigarh with Babbu. Their business had started stabilizing in 2010. And by 2012 we were doing financially well.

After a leisurely breakfast, I was supervising the maid with the cleaning up of the house. Arjun had got a lot of stationery and papers from his office because the place had become infested with rats. He had left in a hurry, and all his stuff was haphazardly lying about. While the maid swept the room, I started putting everything in order. In my head, I was thinking about what to make for dinner that day.

I had no idea that I was going to get the biggest shock of my life a few moments later.

I found his book of verses first. Initially, I thought that it was a compilation Arjun had printed from the internet, but when I read the introduction, the rug was pulled from under my feet. Dazed, I started rummaging through the rest of the stationery . . . and got an even bigger shock.

I found this book lying under some papers.

Immediately, I sent the maid away and sat down to read through the two books. Sanghmitra came to the room to talk to me, but I asked her to go away. The second time she came, I shouted at her.

I finished reading both the books within four hours. To say that I was shattered would be an understatement. My whole world had crumbled around me in a few hours. To learn that the man I loved, my husband, the father of my daughter, had been in love with a married woman, a woman I was fond of and very close to, was so painful I cannot even begin to describe it in words. I was sick, suffocated, and furious.

I had always considered Arjun as my own property, one on whom I had infinite right. He who was my whole world . . . but now suddenly he seemed thousands of miles away.

Arjun had hidden his financial truth from me for years. He had heard some very harsh words from me and our relatives for years. He had been disgraced at parties and family functions. His dignity had been questioned. Now, had he become so shameless that he had cheated on his wife, his daughter, his family with the wife of his friend? It was disgusting.

Arjun was expected to return that same evening. How was I going to face him? What was I going to say to him? What would his reaction be? You see these things in movies, you read about them in papers, you hear about them from friends, but you never think that this may happen to you too. So when life plays an ugly game with you, you are absolutely clueless as to how you should respond to it.

I felt like screaming at God. I imagined that the powers that be were laughing at me. I imagined that the whole society was laughing at me. Where had I lacked? Something had gone horribly wrong somewhere. But where and what?

My head was a whirlpool of questions and doubts and complaints and confusion. I did not know what to do, whom to talk to, where to go, how to handle it, and, most importantly, why—why had it all happened?

Just then, the doorbell rang. My heart started pounding.

Had Arjun come earlier than expected? My mind became blank.

Trembling, I walked to the door and opened it. To my relief, it was only the courier wallah.

He handed me an international mail.

A coincidence from Finland.

A letter sent by Tamanna.

It was a registered letter for Arjun. Postmen do not give these letters to anyone but the person they are addressed to. But this postman was known to us. He had been distributing letters in the locality for more than twenty years. So when I insisted, he gave me the letter. .

I ran to the bedroom and tore open the blue envelope. At that time, I didn't care that it was addressed to Arjun and I should not be opening it. A lot of things had remained hidden from me for far too long. I did not want any more secrets.

Tamanna's letter unveiled a reality that changed everything. My mind started spinning, and I had to lie down in order to breathe properly.

It was then that it struck me that I was in my lowest life state—a state of anger. According to Buddhism, the worst emotion a person can express is anger, because it is the enemy of all rationality and logic. Anger makes you vulnerable and makes you blind to your faults. It makes you perform actions that you go on to regret for your whole life.

For the next couple of hours, I prayed non-stop—for strength and endurance to survive the biggest test of my life and for wisdom to be able to react in the right away.

When the doorbell rang again a few hours later, I knew it

would be Arjun. I walked to the door in a stupor and found him standing there with a smile, which disappeared the moment he saw me. Without saying a word, I turned around and trudged to the study room. The two books were lying on the bed. Behind me, Arjun stopped the moment he realized what had happened. I pushed the letter into his hands and sat down at the edge of the bed, mute and unmoving. A short while later, Arjun sat down next to me and placed his hand on my arm.

Both of us started sobbing.

We lost count of the minutes and hours. Neither of us could speak anything though there was so much we could have said. We communicated our pain, our complaints, and our apologies through the language of tears.

A long time later, there was a call on the landline. Arjun went out to answer it.

He returned to the room a minute later to tell me that one of my cousins had passed away after a cardiac arrest. We had to leave for the funeral immediately.

We didn't speak a word to each other on our way to my relatives' house. Surprisingly, instead of thinking about the earthquake that had shook the foundations of my life only some hours ago, I was thinking of the cousin whose funeral we were going to.

I had never been close to him. He was sixteen years elder to me and was closer to my mother in age than me. After my father expired, we were short of funds and my mother had to seek shelter at our relatives' place. Many people in the family came forward to help us. They all insisted that we stay with them till our situation became better. They offered their home, hearth, and hospitality. If we stayed at one place for a long time, others would complain. So we found ourselves shifting from one address to another.

For two weeks, we stayed at that cousin's place too. Initially, it went well . . . but soon, things started becoming unpleasant. My mother was a twenty-nine-year-old widow and I was her young fatherless daughter. We were alone and unsupported in a world full of cruel strangers and evil friends—the cousin would repeatedly make us aware of this and murmur of sympathy. But his sympathies slowly became excuses to come close to my mother. He would sit with her and touch her arm or shoulder or face. Sometimes, he would keep his hand above her knee. My mother was scared and broken and did not protest . . . until he went too far.

One day, when we were all home, he tried to force himself on her. My mother shoved him away and shouted at him. He stormed out of the room. We left the house the next day.

That was only the first in a series of ugly incidents that happened with my mother. It is easy for a young, lonely widow to find sympathy, but it is as easy for her to find men who want to take advantage of her. My mother recounted all the horrors to me two years before I got married. She told me she had been groped by her uncles, misbehaved with by my father's brothers, and insulted, blamed, and hushed by the society.

On our way back home, I broke the silence between me and Arjun.

"You had a nervous breakdown in Chandigarh because of her?"

Arjun faintly nodded, his eyes glued to the road, his hands firmly holding the steering wheel.

"Where did I go wrong, Arjun?"

A tear rolled down his cheek. He still did not look towards me. After some moments, he croaked, "I can't say sorry. But, I assure you I never—"

I interrupted him. "I know. I read your book."

We barely spoke to each other for the rest of the day. We had to attend a relative's wedding that evening. It had been finalised months ago and involved huge amount of money. Therefore, despite the death, it did not get cancelled. The two families were not closely related to each other anyway.

In the state we were in, we would have gladly given it a miss. But it was important to attend it, so we halfheartedly got ready and reached the venue. The father of the bride was my distant cousin uncle. The wedding card had said that the baraat would arrive at 9. We reached the venue around 10.30, like everyone in Delhi does. But there was no sign of the baraat even then.

We had dinner and met other relatives. It was difficult to show our happy faces to them, but we somehow managed it. The next time I checked my watch, it was midnight. The baraat was yet to make an appearance. Most of the guests had left and even those who had remained behind were getting fidgety.

It was at 12:30 when we heard the procession in the distance, and it was a little after 1:00 that the baraat reached the gates. What happened after that was something no one had ever expected.

The groom's cousins were drunk and started misbehaving with the serving staff. One of the brothers slapped a waiter. The women started complaining about the arrangements, even though they were absolutely lavish and flawless. Arguments broke out between the two sides. To appease everyone, my uncle had to apologize to the groom's father. It was ridiculous. Later, I saw him sobbing in an inner room. He was worried about his daughter's future.

We returned home around three o'clock and went to bed without any discussion. I couldn't sleep after all that I had witnessed in the last twenty-four hours.

My dilemma regarding Arjun was becoming more and more complicated. One minute, I'd be mad at him and feel betrayed and abused. But the next minute, I'd feel worried for him. To realize that he had suffered a mental breakdown without my knowledge made me feel guilty and concerned. He had constantly stayed by me while I had gone through a rough patch in 2003. But I had been unable to even see what he was going through for years.

For hours, I sat pondering why it had all happened. The best answer I could come up with was that the discord that had entered our relationship after 2006 had somewhere left a gap that Tamanna filled. Of course, Arjun denied it in his book, but I felt that either Arjun did not realize this or that he did not want to admit it.

This did not justify his action in any way of course. If there are cracks in your marriage, you are supposed to work on mending them, and not go and obsess over your friend's wife, for God's sake.

Two days later, we received some tragic news that made me pause and think. It brought everything in perspective. My uncle, the one whose daughter's wedding we had attended, had passed away due to a heart attack. Apparently, he had been extremely worried and anxious about his daughter's future. The groom's family had showed their true colours only after it had gotten too late to make amends.

***

I know what you have been thinking while reading this book. How did Sangini ever become okay with the fact that her husband fell in love with another woman outside their marriage? It's hard to believe, isn't it? After all, trust and faithfulness form the backbone of any relationship, and if they are broken, what is left?

But you know what I think? My husband is better than most other men in the world.

I concluded this the day I learnt about my uncle's death. I felt absolutely horrified to learn that a father had to die because of the insolence and inconsiderateness of some men and women. My uncle had spent months preparing for the wedding, and the groom's side spoiled everything in a matter of few minutes.

Tell me who is better? My husband or the groom's uncles and brothers?

When Arjun and I used to go for morning walks, I would notice that most men, from the youngest to the oldest, would scan me and every other woman from head to toe as they went around with their wives. Arjun, however, never looked at other women, no matter how attractive they looked. I have noticed him many times when we are in public. His eyes never wander.

Tell me who is better: my husband or the millions of committed men who mentally undress every woman walking down the street?

Women are unsafe not only outside their homes but even inside. How many women do you know who have been groped and harassed at home by their sundry relatives? I know many of them. I have heard uncountable horror stories not only from my mother but also from my friends and cousins. Arjun, however, treats my mother and other relatives with utmost respect. He has never made any distinction between my mother and his.

Tell me who is better: men who abuse women they should protect or my husband who treats every woman humbly and courteously?

Then, there are husbands who ignore their wives, who

disrespect them, who abuse them, even hit them. Most men think they are superior to their wives and treat their life-partners subordinately. Unlike all these men, Arjun treats me as his equal. He has always been by my side, has always loved and cared for me. I know in my heart that he can never hurt me intentionally. He never even allows me to cross the road without holding my hand and carefully guiding me through the traffic. He loses all appetite if I am unwell. He starts feeling cold in the peak summer months and sleeps with the fan off if I have cold.

He fell in love with Tamanna, I know, but he never really cheated on me with her. His love was pure and platonic. There are men out there who regularly cheat on their wives, without their wives ever coming to know. My husband is not one of them. He can never be one of them.

We all err in life. Even I must have made some mistakes. When I learnt about Arjun's financial truth, I said some really harsh words to him, while he silently listened, regretful and apologetic.

I could have asked Arjun what he would have done if I had fallen in love with Sanjay and wrote a book of verses dedicated to him. But I didn't, for I already knew the answer. I knew the answer from the time before we met Tamanna.

While I sometimes cursed Arjun for failing to provide for me and my daughter financially, he would say he wished I met a man who could give me all the luxuries. He failed as a husband, he felt that way. "I pray from the bottom of my heart for a wonderful man in your life. Somebody who could fulfill his duties and give you a comfortable and dignified life. I am wasting the best days of your life," he would say. For him the important thing was that I stay happy, not that I stay with him. His love was selfless, not selfish.

That I think is true love. And this is why my husband is a far better man than all the men I know. I am proud of him. He is not a cheater, he is not a womanizer. He is a loving and caring husband and an affectionate, dutiful father. And that is why I love him.

Before I end, I must say something about the woman this book is dedicated to. Tamanna . . . I have no bad feelings for her. I can only imagine how difficult it must have been for her to stay away from Arjun after he confessed his feelings for her. She maintained a dignified distance from my husband and even guided him towards the right path. She was a rare woman, and honestly, it's a consolation that Arjun fell in love with her and not some ordinary, unexceptional woman.

After his first book, Arjun struggled to write his second book for a long time. All of us prayed for him—Tamanna, me, and Arjun himself. He wanted to write a love story. And I think Tamanna was the universe's way of giving him a great love story to write. A power greater than us out there wanted to put this book on earth, and it orchestrated this miracle through Tamanna. That is what I think. And that is why I delivered this book to the publishers with my own hands . . .

TAMANNA'S LETTER

Dear Arjun,

Forgive me please. Please forgive me because I may not be able to seek apology again. I am going . . . I tried your phone many times, but the connection failed. My severely numbered moments can't wait for luck anymore. So dearly I wanted to hear your voice one last time. But maybe this is my punishment for the hurt that I caused you . . .

It was all quite strange. For years together we knew each other as acquaintances and then finally we became friends. Somehow, I always felt connected to you by some strong force

You always seemed to be my own . . . I felt a sense of belonging towards you . . . I loved you . . .

I tried to push back my emotions but failed many times

I always wanted to see you happy. I knew you were in deep pain. I could feel that. And I always had this strong desire to encourage you and see you succeeding in life.

Whenever I looked at myself in the mirror, my own being appeared highly shameful to me. How could I think the way I was thinking about you? This question always haunted my conscience. I always felt as if Sangini was staring deep into my eyes accusingly.

When we talked to each other, you and I, I had a lot of fun. On many occasions I disconnected the phone on some pretext or the other because I felt that if I spoke to you for long, I would lose control on myself and my life with my husband and son would shatter.

Yet I loved you . . . and always will. . . . I understand it's wrong to be in love with someone else when you are married yourself and the other person too is married . . .

But the day you shared your heart with me over the phone, I experienced unparalleled happiness. How could this be true, I wondered . . . as if somebody up there in heaven had decided everything. But after serious introspection, I understood that we had to be wise.

Then, after two days, I received a mail from Babbu with your book of poetry attached with it.

Oh Arjun . . . why did you do that? You shook my soul from deep within. You stirred my whole existence. I read the book and I just collapsed. I simply collapsed, Arjun. Each word of those verses was like a divine kiss for me. I felt as if now I was complete. Words will never be sufficient to express the magnitude of happiness that I experienced that day. But quite strangely, that very same night, I dreamt of Sangini. It was a dream best left undescribed but it helped me gain back my lost sense of reality.

I had to be harsh on you and myself as well. I fold my hands in deep apology, my dear, but I had to do that. It was a lovely, mysterious happening, but moving forward even an inch would have been a disaster for everyone. After reading the verses I knew that it would be impossible to have a normal relationship with you. Sangini is a gem of a person and I never wanted to cause any misery to Sanjay as well.

It was good fortune that Sanjay decided to move to Finland with his brother. Otherwise things would have been difficult.

I had to be wise, Arjun. I had to be wise, for your happiness and for mine as well. I hope you will forgive me for hurting you . . . I am sorry.

God, I fell in love . . . But now I have no fear and no regret. I am taking your memories to the other world. We will meet certainly, in some other life time. Please seek permission from my dearest Sangini on my behalf, to allow me to stay with you at least for one full life time. I promise

I won't hurt you . . . I would never hurt you again . . . it was all destiny, my dear, but only for this lifetime.

Regret will always remain in my heart of not being able to do justice to the verses that were written for an unworthy person like me. But we will meet again soon, Arjun. Soon I am about to meet God, and will strongly persuade him to give you all the success and fame that you deserve.

Want to keep writing more . . . and more but my fingers are shaking.
Let me end this letter with a small verse from my side:
Could you come and give some nourishment to my soul?
I have been fasting through my eyes since ages.
Please wait for another lifetime, Arjun . . . We will surely meet.

Warm regards and love . . .
Tamanna

She died in a car accident, thousands of miles from me. The letter was written on January 6th 2010. She had given it to a nurse in her last moments. The writing was broken, as if written from an extremely shaky hand. Soon after, the nurse got transferred to another hospital and lost the letter in her own belongings during shifting her home.

But she found it in a book two years later. My address was on the envelope, so she wasted no time in mending her mistake. She added another letter with it, stating her short story.

Inherently curious about relationships and mysteries surrounding human emotions, Tejeshwar Singh runs a software consultancy firm in Delhi. He was a little late in realizing his passion towards creative writing, but doesn't regret it. This is his second book and was almost auto-writing—it emerged from the deepest confines of his sub-conscience. His first book, *I've Had Enough . . . God!!!*, was published by Rupa in 2009.